ALPHA'S FIRE

A DRAGON SHIFTER ROMANCE

RENEE ROSE
LEE SAVINO

Copyright © March 2022 Alpha's Fire by Renee Rose and Lee Savino

All rights reserved. This copy is intended for the original purchaser of this e-book ONLY. No part of this e-book may be reproduced, scanned, or distributed in any printed or electronic form without prior written permission from the author. Please do not participate in or encourage piracy of copyrighted materials in violation of the author's rights. Purchase only authorized editions.

Published in the United States of America

Midnight Romance, LLC

This e-book is a work of fiction. While reference might be made to actual historical events or existing locations, the names, characters, places and incidents are either the product of the author's imaginations or are used fictitiously, and any resemblance to actual persons, living or dead, business establishments, events, or locales is entirely coincidental.

This book contains descriptions of many BDSM and sexual practices, but this is a work of fiction and, as such, should not be used in any way as a guide. The author and publisher will not be responsible for any loss, harm, injury, or death resulting from use of the information contained within. In other words, don't try this at home, folks!

WANT FREE BOOKS?

Go to http://subscribepage.com/alphastemp to sign up for Renee Rose's newsletter and receive a free books. In addition to the free stories, you will also get special pricing, exclusive previews and news of new releases.

Download a free Lee Savino book from www.leesavino.com

PROLOGUE

Tabitha, age 18

THE CHILLY AIR nips my skin, bared by my tank top. An hour into my hike, I've already shed my jacket—I'm a strange combination of cold and sweaty. Weird, but it feels good.

There's snow on the peaks towering ahead of me. It's spring here, but snow still lingers in the long shadows of the thickly clustered pines.

This early in the morning, my breath puffs as I trek across a frozen field where a few yellow wildflowers poke their heads up over the matted grass. I'm the only tourist crazy enough to be hiking so early in the season. I haven't seen anyone on the trail.

The mountains of northern Italy are technically the Alps, but the locals call them *I Dolomiti*. The hike I chose isn't as challenging as the ones that would carry me up the tallest peak, but my thighs burn from the steady incline. It's still better than swaying down a catwalk in five-inch heels and a weird poofy dress that left most of my back and butt uncovered. When I was a model, I'd do anything for fashion but no longer. This model has officially quit the circuit.

"I don't understand," my mother wailed when I called to tell her. "You were doing so well. You were making such great contacts." In mom-speak, that meant I was meeting men. Rich men who'd love to have a model on their arm. The sort of man my mom hoped would sweep me off my feet and give me a diamond ring and marriage proposal or at least a diamond watch and an extended stay in his private penthouse. Maybe even a car and a few trips to the Riviera or Seychelles.

The type of man my mother always chased after.

I didn't tell her that it was my date with exactly that kind of man that broke me. I was at another boring after-party on the arm of a short stock broker named Paul. Perfectly nice guy, but just because I'm a model and his head barely clears my shoulder doesn't mean that he has the right to put his hand on my ass.

I've stomped across the meadow and up the trail that's disappearing between the blue-gray pines before I realize I'm muttering under my breath. A bird trills on an evergreen branch above my head, and my rage disappears.

I take a moment to clear my lungs. The air is fresh and better than any expensive cologne. The water flowing from a mountain stream is pure snowmelt and probably tastes like heaven. Tiny purple flowers peek up from the cracks in the gray rocks, and the bird above my head warbles like his sex life depends on it.

I'm far from the fashion circuit in Milan. No more crowded events that overwhelm my senses. No more clashing auras or toxic energies leaving me with a headache, desperate to get away.

No more handsy businessmen who treat me like a cigar—a possession, an indulgence, a prop. No more sharing an apartment with six other half-starved young people whose daily food intake adds up to barely half a sandwich. The first thing I did after I told my agent I quit was eat a giant bowl of cheesy pasta.

Right now, my backpack is full of the best provisions: good cheese, a local red wine, and several packs of biscotti.

I may have disappointed my mother, but I feel better than I have in a year. Like a weight lifted off my chest.

It's been almost three months since I quit and started wandering like a vagabond. I spent a little of my fashion week earnings on a pair of hiking boots and a backpack. The rest of my nest egg has gone to reserving the little mountain huts called *rifugios* and a nice rental near Lake Como where I stayed while waiting for the snow to melt.

The plan is to hike Alta Via 1 and beyond. Spend the summer in the mountains. And after that, who knows? I'm eighteen, and I can do anything. This spring is the start of my new life.

Fifteen minutes of climbing, and my thighs are shaking, but it's all worth it when I round the corner and come across a magical mountain lake. The water is a brilliant teal, an ethereal color as bright and shocking as a Lilly Pullitzer jumper.

I can't resist going to the edge and dipping my hand in, but instead of bracing cold, the water is warm as a freshly drawn bath. In the middle of the lake, steam's rising off the surface.

Is this a hot spring? If so, my guidebook didn't mention it.

I drop my jacket and my pack. Facing the clear pool, I feel extra grimy. I'm so tempted to strip everything off and jump in.

But I'm not alone.

There's a man in the pool. His dark head is even with a rocky outcropping, which is why I didn't see him before.

Once I see him, I can't look away. He's not swimming, but walking in the shallows. Water streams off his sculpted shoulders, lapping lovingly at his massive pectoral muscles.

A few more steps towards the shore, and water flows away from his diamond-hard abs, cut and sculpted with the precision of a jeweler. He's got the height and frame of a bodybuilder, but something about the hollows under his high cheekbones and the lean sinew of his arms and chest tells me he is thirty to forty pounds underweight.

My God. I've been in Milan around some of the hottest male models in the world, and they look like Play-Doh figurines next to this guy. Dark brows. Long, silky lashes, thick black hair. His wild beard is a little out of control, but I don't mind. How would it feel between my legs?

The man turns, and the sunlight catches his eyes. They're a stunning amber color. Then they fall on me and heat to molten gold.

"Oh excuse me," I step back. "I didn't mean to intrude."

The man stares at me and makes a noise between a grumble and a growl, and the earth moves in an answering rumble. I lurch as the ground shakes.

Are we having an earthquake? Or did the earth move when our eyes met? Goosebumps break out over my body. The man is still staring at me, and I can't look away.

He's coming up out of the pool. Water streams off his perfect body, running in rivulets down his Adonis belt–the cut muscles making a V pointing straight to his groin. If he comes out of the water a little bit further, I'll be able to see his...

Oh yes, there it is. And damn if he's a shower, not a grower.

Except actually... He is a grower. Because the longer I stare at his cock, the bigger it gets.

"Holy hell," I mutter. This wild man in the wilderness with a beard like John the Baptist is making me hotter and wetter between my legs than I've ever been. Maybe I'm just in a dry spell. In Milan, I was never tempted. The male models were beautiful, but they were also coke-headed man whores. This guy could outshine them all–and he's lighting my fire in a way that I never expected.

The man opens his mouth and says something in a thick accent my brain tries and fails to decipher.

"*Che cosa?*" *What?* I ask in Italian. I frantically try to remember my meager French or Spanish, or any language really. The musical sound is nothing like the Italian I learned in the city. Maybe it's a local dialect?

The man speaks again, another long string of beautiful syllables rolling from his mouth like poetry. His voice is deep and rich.

Golden light flashes around his head and disappears. I blink. This guy doesn't have an aura. Usually I see auras like a subtle glow around a person and sometimes even the stuff they own. I pick up on their emotional energy too–at the fashion shows the cacophony of feelings could make me nauseous.

But this stranger's energy is not intrusive. His aura is clear–or hiding. His emotional presence is a void or so subtle it blends seamlessly with my energy. I've never felt anything like it.

It makes him strangely enticing. Too bad everything else about him screams *Psycho!*

Around him, the lake bubbles, steam rising in a curtain between us.

Is the water boiling around him?

The ground moves and rumbles again. It must be an earthquake.

I step back and lick my lips so I can speak. "I probably should be going…"

The man stalks forward. He's speaking the same phrase over and over again.

I back away. Not because I'm getting full-on psychopath vibes, not because he looks like he's going to murder me and leave my body on the side of the mountain, but because he's looking at me like he's a dying man, and I'm his savior.

He holds out a large, bronzed hand. Even from a distance, I sense the heat coming off his palm as if he has hot coals under his skin.

But that's crazy.

The earth shakes, and I almost lose my balance. My pack and jacket are a few feet away, but I've already backed up to the tree line. Overhead, the trunks and branches creak.

On the peak above the lake, the limestone cracks. Rocks the size of my backpack tumble down in dusty streams. Some sort of avalanche is happening, and I should be running for my life.

Instead, I stare back at the gorgeous bronze god stepping out of the pool. His tone has changed, his voice becoming less musical and more guttural. A growl that echoes around the lake and seems to trigger more falling rocks.

A tree branch whips my face and breaks our eye contact, and it's like weights have fallen off my feet. I turn and scramble down the trail.

A primordial roar shakes the trees and almost knocks me off my feet. I fly down the trail, my legs pumping and my arms flailing, my body half falling and out of control. My heart careens around my chest, bursting with painful adrenaline. I can't get the man's eyes out of my head. It feels like he's right behind me, about to catch up.

A great blast of wind gusts over me and sends me careening into a brace of mugo pine. I grab the trunks and hold on. Rocks bounce over the dirt. The earth is shaking like gravity's about to throw me off.

The taller trees' branches thrash the air like a great hurricane has blown up. A giant wind, an earthquake and a tornado all rolled into one. The air high above ripples, and another roar blasts the trees and sends more rocks crashing down from their heights.

I hug the earth and crawl until I make it to a thick cluster of Norway pines. The earthquake has stopped, but great gusts of wind roll through the forest, tearing at the trees and flattening the flowers and long grasses in the meadows. A great shadow appears, gliding over me, blocking out the sun and disappearing as fast as it came.

I don't know how I make it down the mountain. When I get to the village, I'm still shaking. I've lost my backpack and my jacket. When I try to explain in broken Italian what happened, the locals look at me like I'm crazy. No one else experienced an earthquake or a hurricane.

I don't mention the man to anyone. His presence remains my secret.

I give up on my plans to hike the Dolomites, and head south to Tuscany instead. After two weeks of looking over my shoulder, I've convinced myself the event never happened. It was a dream. Some sort of vision, my psychic powers going berserk. I stepped on a funny mushroom, inhaled some psychedelic spores, and bam! Hallucinated a crazy sexy man and a weird weather event.

But, over the years, some nights I wake with a start, my

chest flushed and my core throbbing from the recurring dream. He comes to me in my sleep, the man I've tried to forget. Wild hair, amber eyes, speaking a beautiful cascade of poetry in a language only my heart understands.

And every time, I wake with the strangest sense that he's the only thing that's real, and the rest of my life is the dream.

1

Ten years later…

GABRIEL

I stare down at the sleeping angel in my castle. Her caramel-colored hair fans out from her head on the soft goose-down pillow I had covered in a scarlet linen for her. She's not in my bed–not yet.

I had a room of her own made up for her, so she'd feel more comfortable in her new surroundings. Her new home. She'll move into my tower bedroom with me once she's used to me. But I thought it was important that she have her own space during our courtship.

She stirs, and every cell in my body electrifies. Smoke billows from my nostrils, my dragon celebrating her presence as much as I do.

She's really here. After searching for ten years, I've found her.

The one female on the planet who belongs to me. The one who will make me whole again. My mate.

She's not a dragon in this lifetime. She wasn't in the last one, either.

No, fate gifted me with a delicate human flower. A cruel twist that nearly destroyed me last time. Drove me underground to slumber for hundreds of years.

But my sweet Tabitha woke me from my sleep, and I scoured the edges of the Earth to find her. Now I have her here, in my lair.

My beautiful bride.

I have this second chance, and I won't let any harm come to her this time. That's why I lured her away from the wolves she runs with. I couldn't chance any interference. I needed to get her to my castle where I can keep her safe. Protect her with my soldiers, not my dragon.

But, of course, he came out the moment I caught her scent in the wind. The pure joy of being near her again created chaos within me. I changed form, and when Tabitha saw my fiery side, she fainted.

I need to take care with her. Keep my reptilian eyes covered with sunglasses and the dragon in the cave until she's ready. Let her get used to me first, to fall in love and feel secure before I show her the beast.

I plan to court her properly. Show her my treasures. The armies under my command. The beautiful castle where she will reside. I have had a millennia to amass everything it takes to dazzle and woo her.

I lean over to fill my nostrils with her scent. Honeysuckle and spring. Morning dew. I lightly trace the outline of her rosebud lips. So perfect. It's no wonder she was paid to show off designers' garments in her youth. Countries go to war over women like her.

Now no man will lay his eyes on her unless I allow it. If I wish, I will lock her in my tower and keep her as one of my treasures.

I'm tempted to do it now… but no. I am committed to winning Tabitha's affections. Her love. Although I'd prefer to lock her in a cage, allowing her out only when I wish to breed her…

A delicate clearing of the throat calls my attention to the door, where Buttons, my butler stands, impeccably dressed, as always, in his coat tails and cumberbund.

"Forgive the intrusion, sir, but Mr. Hess says you have a meeting scheduled with him."

I don't wish to tear my gaze from my sleeping bride, but Buttons is right. My head of security awaits to be briefed on how I plan to keep Tabitha safe. It's important.

"Thank you, Buttons. I will be right there."

I allow myself one more touch of my treasure's silky hair and leave.

Tabitha

My face is pressed to a silken cloud. Did my bed become extra comfortable last night? Even the sheets feel softer. The mattress embraces me like it's molded to my form.

I crack my eyes and try to move. I feel like I slept for a couple of years.

The room around me is dark, but automatically, I know it's not home. I'm not in my cute converted train car where I live in Taos, New Mexico.

Where am I? My brain is slow to come online. Why can't I remember how I got here?

The bed is huge. My bed back home is way smaller, and it's not surrounded by a thick brocade curtain that cocoons the king-sized bed in shadow. The drapes hang from a four-poster frame and even cover the top. It's a rich red and gold tapestry the likes of which I've seen in antique auctions that I frequent.

Is that gold thread? I sit up to examine it and pull open the curtain to peek out. I'm in a massive stone room with more red and gold Turkish rugs. The thirty-foot-high ceiling has thick wooden rafters like some sort of medieval great hall.

Did I hit my head? Am I in some sort of hotel, and I don't remember checking in?

I was on a road trip headed to a jewelry show. I had a few antique auctions to stop at along the way.

My head is muzzy like I took a sleeping pill. I rub my face. There's something I was supposed to do...

I reach for my phone, but it's gone. I'm wearing my peasant skirt and a loose white blouse, but my well-worn Birkenstocks are missing.

My hair is down and in a smooth sheet. Not in my usual braid, but it's unsnarled for once. I must have slept solidly, with no dreams or thrashing around.

My heart starts to pick up speed when I can't figure out how I got here. I mean, sometimes when I travel it takes me a minute to remember where I am, but this time it's just not coming back.

What happened to me?

The last thing I remember, I was headed to a special estate sale in my pink VW bus. The directions took me to the middle of nowhere.

The rest is all muzzy.

I pull back the curtains in preparation to swing out of bed. My legs are wobbly and weak, so I give myself a second.

On the far left wall is a bank of ancient-looking windows. I can't see anything more than sky–the glass is old and warped and looks bounded by lead. Between me and the windows is a space that would fit my whole Taos home. Instead of bean bag chairs and lava lamps, there are antique chairs upholstered in red velvet and a massive stone fireplace decorated with snarling gargoyles.

This hotel's really going with the medieval gothic theme. All that's missing is a suit of armor in the corner.

Everything is clean at least. And warm–there's an actual fire in the fireplace. A bluish flame dances along modern-looking sculpture, but faint black scorch marks on the stone tell me this was used as a fireplace long before it was updated to a gas-fed fire.

To the right of the bed is what looks to be a bathroom. I stumble into it on shaky legs. The bathroom is just as cavernous, and they kept the medieval castle theme with the exception of modern plumbing. The pool-sized bathtub is set into the stone floor. Even more tempting is the steam shower, a wonder of technology with so many buttons and nozzles I might need an engineering degree just to figure out how to turn it on.

I settle for splashing water on my face. The towels are a dream, white and plushy. *Four out of five stars. Minus one for the weird castle vibe.*

There's a door off the bathroom. Soft overhead lights go on, revealing dresses, blouses, skirts, and jeans hanging in neat rows between floor-to-ceiling shelves holding pairs and pairs of gorgeous shoes. Whose?

I finger the closest item, a knee-length silken caftan in teal, the color of Lake Como. There are no weird women's business suits with shoulder pads or sensible black skirts. Or worse, tight club wear, the sort my mom thinks I should wear to land a hedge fund billionaire boyfriend. Everything in here is designer, but something I'd wear. It's like a genie cataloged everything I've ever loved to wear and created the closet of my dreams.

I grab a pair of Gucci jeans and hold them against my front. Yep, my size. So are the pairs of Sophia Webster and Valentino heels, and Frye and Zadig & Voltaire boots, all displayed in their own backlit cubbies, like they're in a Milan storefront. I don't wear high heels often, but for the whimsical butterfly design or rockstar studded leather, I'd make an exception.

I clutch a red leather riding boot to my chest. I should put it back in its cubby, but I'm barefoot in a strange place. Maybe I can borrow some footwear. I don't know whose room I ended up in, but she does have great taste.

I find a pair of thin socks and tug on the boots. They fit perfectly.

In a daze, I step out of the closet and stop short. The massive wooden and leather studded bedroom door is still closed, but I'm no longer alone.

A tall man stands by the fireplace, his head bowed as he regards the fire. He turns as if sensing my presence. He's in a dark suit--Brioni by the look of it–and there's something familiar about him. The close-cropped beard lining the strong line of his jaw, the dark hair falling across his forehead. He's wearing a pair of oversized sunglasses that hide the middle half of his face. The lenses are totally black.

"You are awake, my treasure," he says in accented English.

My treasure? Uh...do I know you?

His accent rolls around in my head. Where have I heard it before? I take a step forward. "Where am I? Who are you? What is happening?"

He waits until I fall silent. "Patience, Tabitha. In time, I will answer every question you have."

The unease I'd been trying to keep at bay filters into

my bloodstream. This is getting weirder by the second. "You know my name."

"I know everything about you."

Goosebumps race down my arms. *That's not creepy at all.* I should run for the door, but something keeps my feet rooted to the spot. The man seems relaxed and in charge. There's nothing menacing about him, and for some reason, I'm fascinated by him rather than frightened. "Are you the hotel manager?"

The corner of his perfect lips twitches. "No."

"What is this place?"

"You're in my home."

His home.

What?

"And how did I get here?" I wrack my brain for memories of the night before, but I still don't remember anything beyond driving in the middle of nowhere in my VW bus.

"I had you brought here after you passed out."

"I passed out?" My yelp echoes off the stone walls.

"I had a doctor examine you. He found you perfectly healthy, other than some minor fatigue and dehydration."

I press a hand over my heart. I've never passed out, even when living off green smoothies and a handful of raw almonds on the modeling circuit. "No. I don't pass out. That doesn't make sense."

"Be at ease, Tabitha," he says in that deep rolling voice of his. It's strangely soothing. I'm sensitive to people's bad vibes, but I'm at ease with him. Memory tugs at me. Do I recognize him from somewhere?

A tiny fork of lightning appears around his head, thin as spider web. Like a floating golden thread. It disappears instantly, leaving nothing where the man's aura should be.

I was young when I realized not everyone could see colors around people the way I could. I was in the park and kept pointing to peoples' heads, babbling to my mom about the blue, yellow, or red colors around them. She smacked my hand and told me to be quiet.

Now I don't talk about my visions with anyone, ever. Not even my friends. I learned early on that they make people uncomfortable. So I keep silent and use my gifts to navigate the world.

This guy has no aura. I can't sense him psychically. It's relaxing. Like putting on noise-canceling headphones during a Schoenberg concert. Blissfully quiet.

And something about him seems so familiar...

The stranger speaks again. "If you like, I can summon the doctor again."

"No, that's okay. I feel fine now." I don't like that a doctor examined me, and I didn't even wake up. Something is off here. Way off.

"I had the room designed for you." The man blatantly changes the subject.

"For me?" I narrow my eyes. "How do you know me, exactly?"

For a moment, I wonder if this is some kind of blind date my mom cooked up, and he's some uber-rich guy she's sold on marrying me.

But that still doesn't add up. She'd be here, too.

He doesn't answer. Instead, he offers a question of his own. "Do you not like it?"

I shrug. "It would make an interesting Airbnb. A little gothic for my tastes."

"My castle has stood for seven hundred years. I've fully modernized it." He tilts his head to the gargoyles mounted around the fireplace. "But my favorite fixtures remain."

Now that I look closer, the gargoyles look like dragon heads. "Those guys? Do they have names?" I'm being cheeky but this conversation is too surreal.

I don't expect him to answer seriously, but he does, pronouncing two words in a rich, rolling language I don't understand. "*Tragesh and Tradell.* Roughly translates to *Fire Breath* and *Fire Tongue.*"

"What language is that?" I ask, fascinated despite myself. "I don't recognize it, but I feel like I've heard it before."

He tilts his dark head. "Don't you remember, Tabitha? I spoke it to you when we first met."

So I have met this guy. That explains the deja vu, but not why I don't remember him. I would remember being this attracted to someone. "When was that?" I take a few more steps into the room towards him. "Was it in a past life? Because I'm getting a really intense vibe here." I point my finger back and forth between us. My mom would say it's rude to point. She'd also despair about me bringing up any mention of my psychic gifts to a handsome man in a ten thousand dollar suit.

"Perhaps." He doesn't look weirded out. He seems to be considering my question carefully. "Do you believe in past lives?"

I shrug. I don't want to get into my mystical beliefs right now.

"Regardless, the meeting of which I speak happened some years ago," he says. "Ten years ago to be exact."

Ten years ago, I was a model getting ready for fashion week. He's probably some douchebag dude-bro I met at a party, either a model or a designer, or one of the wealthy patrons.

So much for a magical connection. This isn't fate. It's probably kidnapping. This guy is a wannabe James Bond villain and has pulled me into his crazy fantasies.

I need to see his face, his full face. "Do you wear your sunglasses at night?" I ask in a snide tone and regret it when he says, "They are a precaution. But I will remove them when the time is right."

Gah, I should've thought before I spoke. He might have eye issues or photosensitivity. "That was rude. It's none of my business."

"You're wrong, Tabitha. Everything about me is your business. As you are mine."

And now we're right back to creepy stalker territory.

I've walked fully into the bedroom. The door to the hall is a few feet to my right. As much as I want to figure this guy out, my best bet is to get out of here. Get to safety. Run in the red boots and leave the rest of the gorgeous clothes in the closet behind.

To cover up my fluster and my decision, I keep up with the small talk. I point to the bed. "Where did you get that tapestry? I've never seen anything so beautiful. Is it vintage or a remake?"

His head turns. Before he starts talking, I scramble out the door.

A long stone hall greets me. There's a suit of armor. "There goes your four-star rating," I mutter, racing past it. I tug on its arm as I pass. It would be great if it could fall into the middle of the hall and block the way, but it's secured somehow. I can't bring myself to rip down the tapestries lining the rest of the hall. If they are original, they have to be over a hundred years old.

I skid around a corner. More long stone hallway, studded with a few heavy wooden doors. I'm in the bedroom wing of this castle. Must find a staircase. Another hall, another row of doors. In desperation, I try a few of the latches, but they're locked. The windows lining the hall are the same old, thickened glass and banded with lead. Even if I could get one open or break one, there's nothing but sky and a long drop down a sheer stone wall to greet me. This place really is a castle out of a horror movie.

"Negative ten stars. Do not recommend." I leave the bank of windows and rush on. The boots are heavy to be running in. They clomp over the carpet. I should've grabbed a pair of sneakers.

I finally find a staircase leading down ... to a heavy wooden door that's locked. I pound on it, but these doors are a foot thick. I'd need to go all Leatherface on it with a chainsaw.

"Looking for this?" The man stands on top of the stone stairs. He slowly descends, holding up a huge iron key.

It's the point in the horror movie where the heroine screams and dies horribly. But instead of freaking out, I get this intense sense of deja vu.

My heartbeat slows, my heaving lungs calm.

There's just something about this guy. Maybe it's the fact he has no aura or energy infringing on mine. Maybe it's his cologne, a spicy, earthy blend with a touch of smoke. He's close enough that my head tilts back, so I can look up at his face.

"I'm leaving," I say.

He prowls closer. Now I'm surrounded by his spicy, drugging scent. "Don't you want to know who I am? Why I brought you here?" His voice thickens. "Why there's such an affinity between us?"

Actually, I do. "Maybe." I narrow my eyes at him. "But I don't trust you."

"That is wise. You don't know me."

I'm searching the air around his head, looking for his aura. Even I have an aura–I don't see it, but I can sense it. It's typically dark purple.

I've relied on auras for so long to tell me about a

person. This guy has none. It makes me want to rip the glasses off his face, so I can look into his eyes.

"Have dinner with me," he challenges softly.

My stomach growls. The sound is so shocking, I slam my hand over my midriff.

The man's lips compress like he's suppressing a smile. "My butler sets a wonderful table. You can have anything your heart desires."

"Will you answer my questions?"

"Everything you wish to know."

My stomach growls again.

Now there's no trace of a smile on his face. "Tabitha, I cannot bear to see you hungry, tired or hurt. Allow me to be a good host."

We're standing closer now, face to face. His dark shades reflect my curious expression. "Take off your glasses," I say.

"I do not wish to scare you." His tone holds regret.

"Just for a moment. I want to see your face."

Instead of removing the glasses himself, he bows his head. Our breath mingles as I reach up and slide his shades off.

A pair of amber eyes greet me. Familiar amber eyes. Add a few more months of out-of-control growth to his beard and remove the fine suit and...

"It's you." I jerk back so hard I would have hit my head against the wooden door if the man's large hand hadn't cradled it.

"Careful, my treasure." He shifts his body, pinning mine against the door.

There's no mistaking him. This is the man from the mountain. The man I met years ago when I was just eighteen and hiking in the mountains of Northern Italy.

It all comes rushing back: the weird earthquake

shaking the ground as he came towards me, speaking in his foreign tongue. I had dismissed the experience as a hallucination or a dream. Either I didn't eat enough that morning, or my biscotti were spiked with 'shrooms.

But here he is, in the flesh. Solid, real.

Prickles run up my back. "How is this possible?"

He runs his hand down my hair and grips a lock in his fist as if he can't believe I'm real. "I've been searching for a long time."

I inhale more of his incense-like scent. "What's your name?"

"Gabriel." He lifts the lock of my hair to his face and rubs it across his cheek.

"Gabriel," I repeat.

For a moment a gold light flares in his eyes. His pupil seems to become more narrow and slitted. I blink, and his eyes are back to normal.

Gabriel looks like he's going to say more, but a cold restraint settles over his features instead.

"Come now, there's much for you to see." He steps away and fits the key into the lock, turning it until it clicks. The door swings open to a larger, brighter hallway. A rich red carpet lines the stone. He offers his arm. "Shall we?"

2

Gabriel

Too fast. I'm going too fast.

I don't want to frighten my bride.

The truth is, I have no practice in this art. The last time I claimed my mate, I simply arranged the union with her parents. I made my case, proved I was worthy, and, essentially, bought her.

Although she has a mother, Tabitha doesn't seem to be bound by parental oversight. I've learned that in this century, women have free will to roam and travel alone, which is how she, as an off-continent dweller, came to pass over the cave where I slept and woke me ten years ago.

Courtship in this century cannot be that different, though. Her body still responds to mine. I can tell by the way she inhales my scent, the curiosity in her lovely jade gaze.

I would have used the wolf pack she ran with to influence her into marriage, to show her shifters are not to be feared, but as they were my adversaries, I couldn't use that avenue.

Thank fate, I am the sort of creature who enjoys toying with his enemies before he kills them, or I never would have found her on that landmass across the sea. Now, of course, I will not kill the wolf pack. I would never injure those who have given their friendship and cared for my mate.

I lead Tabitha down the red carpet in the window-lined hall. I don't scent fear in her spring rain aroma. Though she's human, I know she senses what I am to her on some level. Her curiosity outweighs her caution, her distrust, with me.

Her gaze keeps drifting up and down my frame, as if she finds it pleasing, but then she averts her gaze when I catch her at it. It feels like she's looking for something she can't find, can't see. We head toward the large, round tower of the castle. Below us is a courtyard surrounded by sheer stone walls as is customary for a medieval fortress.

"Where is this place?" she asks.

"Romania. Transylvania, to be exact."

"Holy shit. You took me to Transylvania?"

"In my private jet."

I watch her closely to see if she's moved by this. Impressed by my means. She is not. She doesn't show me any disdain, but it seems my wealth does not excite her.

Hmm. I will have to discover what makes her tick. Sex, perhaps. Based on those looks she keeps sneaking my way, I believe she finds me attractive.

"Is this Dracula's castle?"

"No. His lies about fifty miles from here."

"That far, huh?"

There's something glib about her remark, but I don't understand it.

I need to find out if she remembers my other form. My dragon. She hasn't mentioned it, which makes me think she's blocked it out. The drugs the doctor gave her may have affected her memory of our meeting.

I hesitate. We traverse the rest of the hall before I say, "I showed you myself, and you were frightened. You fainted."

"Why would I be frightened of you?" she asks easily.

She doesn't remember. She can't.

"You were frightened at our first meeting, too," I remind her. "When you saw me in the Italian Alps."

"That was because you looked like John the Baptist on crack." She steals a glance at my crotch as if remembering how my manhood looked. "I was a single woman hiking alone, I needed to be careful."

"I wouldn't have hurt you. I will never hurt you, Tabitha."

I glide before her to press a fingerprint to a panel on the wall.

"Plus you were *naked,*" she says, her gaze traveling across the breadth of my chest now like she's remembering what I look like unclothed. "And there was that weird storm that blew up…" Her voice dies as I open the doors to my grand ballroom. I take her arm and guide her forward into the grandeur. Here she will get a true impression of my means. Of all that will be hers now.

The ornate painted ceiling is four stories above our heads. Gold and white columns line the walls, breaking up sections of the parquet floor. A poorer king's palace could fit inside this space.

My dragon hates small, confined spaces. Places where I'd have to bust through walls if I shifted. Here, I can shift and still be comfortable.

"Wow," she says. "Throw a lot of parties?" Her voice echoes a little.

"Not for many centuries." Again, I get the sense she's

unimpressed. I try not to worry. Steering her towards a set of gold-framed doors, I take pleasure in simply having her here, by my side. In the privilege of breathing in her honeysuckle scent. I show her another smaller but no less grand hall. The one with columns and walls coated in gold.

"Is that real gold?"

"Yes."

She stops and traces the pattern embossed in the gold–the spiral loops that form a triangle. The same pattern is found on each of my scales. "I like this design," she murmurs like she's more interested in the pattern than the gold. "Borromean rings, right? Three circles that cannot be unlinked. The symbol of unity."

I wait until she's ready to move on. We exit through a normal-sized side door into a set of rooms with tasteful arrays of chaises, desks, and leather armchairs tucked around fireplaces. A long hall runs between them with floor-to-ceiling bookcases filled with my red and gold-bound books. There are even a few rolling ladders.

"Oh my God." Tabitha claps a hand to her forehead like she might swoon. "I may have just had a mini-bookgasm."

I don't understand the word *bookgasm*, but her delight pleases me. Finally, something that impresses my bride.

I guide her forward with the slight pressure of my hand in the small of her slender back. I love touching her. Feeling the gentle slope of her back just above the curves of her glorious ass.

She stops before an ancient globe in a wooden frame. Big as a chair, the globe's surface is yellowed and displays countries that no longer exist.

"This is incredible," she breathes.

"There's more." Enheartened, I take her hand and

press my palm to a security pad, unsealing a special glass area. Inside the temperature and moisture-controlled rooms lies my vast array of ancient maps, displayed carefully.

Tabitha rushes forward to examine them. "Wow. I don't even recognize some of the countries."

"Most of them no longer exist."

"Ooh, you have a map of the Ottoman Empire!"

"Yes, circa 1595."

I let her roam around the room, exclaiming over the ancient artifacts. I make a mental note–not impressed by jets but loves old artifacts. Perhaps that's because she remembers her previous lifetime. The one when she was mine.

Tabitha straightens from examining a scrap of Flemish tapestry. "Are you trying to impress me?"

"Is it working?" I ask. I take her hand and gently lead her out of the room. I would let her stay until she's pored over every item, but I know she's hungry. I carefully seal the room again. It's an old castle, but I've made all the upgrades.

Tabitha presses her lips together like she doesn't wish to admit the truth.

Satisfaction plows through me. She is finally impressed.

She clears her throat as I lead her on through the library. "Will you tell me what you were doing on that mountain top?

"I had woken from a long sleep." I consider saying more but decide against it. If she doesn't remember seeing my dragon, I'm not going to reveal it yet. There's already a lot to take in.

She studies me like she knows I'm holding something back. My bride is as clever as she is beautiful.

"You did scare me," she admits.

"I know. I've regretted it ever since. You ran so fast. I tried to follow, but you disappeared into the village. I had to go back for my clothing, and by the time I returned, you were gone. I looked for you. I have been searching for you these past ten years."

"How did you survive the storm on the mountaintop? The avalanche of rocks?"

The one I caused by shifting into my dragon form? "Easily. You'll find I am difficult to kill."

Tabitha sighs.

"What is it, little one?"

"Each answer you give me only opens up more questions. I'm not sure why I'm playing this game."

"Ah. I do enjoy games. Perhaps you'll come to enjoy playing them with me."

She flips her hair over her shoulder, not in a flirtatious way. She's completely unpretentious and yet, at the same time, as regal as a princess. Quite an enigma.

"I don't like games," Tabitha says. "I'm too straightforward, much to my mother's dismay."

"Oh? Does your mother play games?"

"Only one—attracting and acquiring rich men. She always hoped I'd inherit that talent. She pushed me into anything she thought would help—dance lessons, child beauty pageants, modeling contracts. I rejected it all."

My chest tightens even though I'd already suspected this bit of information. "You don't care for rich men?"

"No. They're too in love with their own power. They like to own their women instead of partner with them, and they're far too controlling."

Something inside me shifts uncomfortably. My dragon doesn't speak to me, yet I sense his judgment. I'm everything she dislikes.

Rich. Powerful. Controlling.

But these are the traits that make me a good mate. What could I offer her without them? She'd be unsafe. Without comforts. Unimpressed.

She's already unimpressed. I push away that uncomfortable thought.

"You say you'll tell me the truth and tell me more about yourself, but everything you say conceals more than it tells me," Tabitha complains.

It's on the tip of my tongue to tell her that is how I prefer to play the game, but she just told me she doesn't like games. I will have to formulate a new plan. In the meantime, I will provide for my mate.

With a wave of my hand, I activate a hidden sensor, and two-story-high double doors glide open to reveal my dining hall. She takes in the massive onyx fireplaces that sandwich a long polished table. The room glows from the light of the fires and the candelabrum on the table. Overhead, a chandelier glistens.

"Isn't this a little overkill?" Tabitha asks, even as her stomach growls loudly. She wavers on her feet, and I catch her elbow to steady her.

"You're famished, my treasure. Please join me at my table."

With my hand at her back, I guide her to the closest end of the table and help her into a high-backed, plush cushioned seat.

"This is like a throne," she muses and nods to the far end of the table. "Are you going to sit on one end of the table, and I sit on the other?"

Something is amusing her, but I'm not sure what. "Is that what you would like?"

She ducks her head to hide a smile. "Maybe."

"Perhaps at another meal." I rest my hand on her nape a moment before I seat myself beside her.

Tabitha

At the end of the room, a door opens, and a man in a tailcoat and white cumberbund enters, wearing a lofty expression. The pinkish haze of his aura clings to his pompadour.

Gabriel waves a hand. "Tabitha, this is my butler, Buttons."

Buttons the butler? Is he serious?

"Pleasure to meet you, madam," Buttons says in a starchy British accent. He unfolds my napkin with a snap and lays it over my lap. "First course tonight is a duck *consommé*."

I sit up straight and try to remember my manners as Buttons leaves the room and returns with a silver tureen.

"This is giving me serious Downton Abbey vibes," I mutter to Gabriel.

He inclines his head but doesn't look like he catches the reference. "Is that a good thing?"

"That remains to be seen."

The broth Buttons ladles into a shallow bowl in front of me smells amazing.

I hazard a guess as to which spoon to use. The salty broth hits my tongue in an explosion of herbed flavor. "Oh my God, that's good." I scrape the bowl in my haste to scoop up more.

Both Buttons and Gabriel are watching me.

I clear my throat. "My compliments to the chef."

"Very good, ma'am. I will pass them along." Buttons swans away, and I relax a little.

Gabriel steeples his fingers, watching me eat with an air of pleasure. "Chef Giampi is very good."

"I hope you're paying him well."

"I pay all my employees well." He dips his head to my bowl. "Does this add to my star rating?"

"You heard that?" I'm down to the last spoonfuls of broth. Would it be rude to pick up the bowl and slurp the rest? "This would be perfect with a grilled cheese sandwich."

"In due time. I told Giampi to start with something light so as not to shock your system. You were asleep for a long time."

"That's so weird. I can't believe I slept through a ride on a private jet."

"I may have had the doctor add a touch of a soporific to the cocktail of vitamins he administered."

I set my spoon down. "Excuse me? Did you just admit to drugging me?"

His dark lashes flutter, but the expression on his handsome face doesn't change. "I will not lie to you."

"That doesn't make it better!"

I glare at Gabriel while Buttons announces and serves a second course. When the butler is gone, I nod to my plate. "Is this drugged?"

"No. I have no need to drug you tonight."

The fucking nerve! If I could shoot fire from my eyeballs and incinerate him, I would.

I use my fork to poke at the cooked carrots. They smell like honey and cumin. My stomach growls. I'm going to need my strength to fight him.

"You would drug me again?" I ask in an icy tone.

"If circumstances required it."

I barely taste the food I'm munching on. At this point, I'm just filling my stomach, so I can regain my strength.

"Why did you drug me the first time?"

"You had fainted. And I thought it best to let you sleep through the journey. You were not harmed. I will never do you harm."

"For the record, roofying me is harming me." I stab a carrot. "What else did you do to me?"

"Other than transport you across an ocean and lay you in a comfortable bed, absolutely nothing."

"You removed my shoes."

"But not your clothes. The first time I undress you, you will have begged for it."

My body has an entirely different reaction to that than my mind. A tightening between my legs. Or is it a loosening? Definitely heat. My visceral reaction to this man and his offensive words confuse me.

I do note that I'm more offended than scared. I still can't find it in me to dredge up a fear response to the knowledge that I've been kidnapped, drugged, and flown across an ocean to Transylvania. Something about this man feels so familiar. Safe.

I respond to that with silence. I give him the silent treatment through the next three courses of the meal.

Gabriel eats sparingly. At some point, the butler serves him some wine from a bottle with an ancient, yellowed label. They don't offer any to me, and I don't ask for any. I don't want to risk upsetting my stomach, and I want all my wits about me.

As soon as I can, I'm gonna blow this joint.

"One thing I don't understand," I say finally, breaking the silence after barely touching the cheese course. "You said I fainted when I saw you. I never faint."

"Circumstances were overwhelming."

"What circumstances?" I concentrate, but I don't

remember. I allow my distress to slip into my voice. "I'm trying not to freak out, Gabriel."

"It is best not to tell you but to show you." He sets his napkin on the plate and rises.

3

Tabitha

"Let us adjourn to the cigar room." Gabriel offers me his hand. I shouldn't allow it, but for some reason, I do. Buttons comes and pulls my chair out for me.

Gabriel's big hand closes gently around mine. My belly is full, and my body comes alive in his presence. I wish I wasn't so damn attracted to this man. I don't understand what's going on. I haven't forgotten that he just admitted to drugging me. Or kidnapping. Or that he's holding me hostage. Yet I still get flutters when he touches me.

He leads me out the way we came. I make note of the twists and turns as we head through the library to a study of some sort.

"So this is the cigar room." Maybe that's where the smoky scent is coming from. But no, the cigars have an earthier scent.

"Yes," Gabriel leaves me standing in front of a large leather sofa and walks to the fireplace. A touch of a button and flames spring to life. "Would you like a cigar?"

"No thanks. They give me headaches." Even with pot. I stick to edibles.

"Does the smoky scent bother you?"

"No. I find it comforting." Some of the rich men my mother chased after smoked cigars. They weren't all horrible assholes. Just most of them.

To the right of us is a bank of windows that overlooks a courtyard the size of half a football field.

"Were all medieval castles this big?" I ask.

"No. Nor was this one when I first conquered it, but I have done many renovations over the years."

"You and your family? You said something about seven hundred years. I assumed you meant your ancestors…"

"No. I meant me."

"I don't understand."

"There are many things that you need to know, and now it is time to tell you. Take a seat," he points to the Chesterfield.

"You know what?" I prop a hand on my hip. "I don't think so. I want to go now."

"Sit down," he orders. His voice is soft but the echo reverberates in my bones.

And I sit. He's got that authoritative voice, the same as Rafe. Rafe can give an order, and you want to obey. I never noticed it until Adele pointed out how she found it annoying as hell.

I glare up at Gabriel like a petulant toddler. "I'd like my phone back. I probably should call my friends." I'd even call my mom.

"Ah, yes, your friends. That is part of what I wish to show you." Gabriel touches another button beside the fireplace, and a fancy flat-screen TV descends from the ceiling. The screen blinks into a familiar view. A stone and timber lodge nestled on a snowy lawn with a pine forest and mountains behind.

I sit up straighter. "That's where Deke lives. Sadie's boyfriend. And Rafe and Channing. Do you have cameras on their house?" My voice bounces off the high ceiling.

Gabriel inclines his head. "I prefer to know where my self-proclaimed enemies reside."

"Rafe is going to go ape shit."

"Rafe Lightfoot, you mean." He hits another button, and there's a picture of Rafe standing on his snow-covered back porch, talking on his cell. "He has yet to spot my falcon drone." Gabriel smirks.

The door behind Rafe glides open, and Adele sticks her head out. Her hair is down and her face is makeup-free. I rarely see Adele like this, and she's my best friend. She's wearing an oversized pair of joggers that pool over her feet and a giant Henley. Rafe's clothes.

"Holy crap, they're together," I gasp. "Is this live footage?"

Gabriel nods. I feel guilty being a voyeur.

Adele says something to Rafe from the door. He ends his call and heads into the house.

The footage changes.

"This is from last night," Gabriel says. There they all are, sitting in the Blue Moon Grill. Deke and Sadie, Lance and Charlie. Charlie is sitting on Lance's lap, his hands are on her thickened belly. Adele and Rafe are both standing and talking to the group like the de facto leaders that they are.

"Stop," I say tiredly. This is just wrong. I can't watch my friend's life like a soap opera. "I need to call them."

"Don't you want to know their secrets? What they've been keeping from you?"

"Whatever it is, I'm sure they had a good reason," I say stubbornly. But now I'm confused and curious.

"You need to know the secrets they're keeping from you. All of them."

"Stop playing these games. Just tell me what's going on, Gabriel."

He ignores me and hits another button, and there's the lodge at night.

"When was this taken?"

"The last full moon."

A chill runs over my skin. The way Gabriel has invaded my friends' privacy is so creepy. I have to tell them. I have to escape.

"Watch," he commands.

There are a few specks of snow swirling down from the sky. The sky is black velvet. A gray and white wolf comes into view, padding across the snowy lawn.

"Holy shit." The wolf is huge. I've seen pictures, but it's another thing to see it in a familiar space and realize how giant wolves are.

The wolf sniffs around the lawn. "So that's their secret?" I roll my eyes. "They have a nature cam?"

The lodge door opens, spilling light over the snow. Out strides Rafe. He's shirtless. No hat or gloves, not even a coat. Adele has talked about how the cold doesn't seem to touch him. She was always obsessed with Rafe, even though she wouldn't admit it.

In the next second, Rafe shucks off his joggers. "Oh, geez." I throw up a hand to block Rafe's form. "That's a naked dick." I'm happy for Adele if she's getting some of that, but I don't want to see it.

"Watch," Gabriel commands.

I peek through my fingers. In one moment, Rafe raises

his leg to take a step into the snow–barefoot. In the next, a massive wolf lands on the bottom stoop.

"What the fuck," I whisper.

The wolf is black with some brownish markings. It bounces over the lawn and lopes off with the first one. A howl rises up off-screen.

Channing and Deke are next. They both walk out undressed the way Rafe was. I don't even try to avert my eyes from their naked forms. Within seconds, they both turn into huge wolves. Deke is a giant black shadow gliding towards the forest. Channing has mostly white fur that blends with the snow.

"I can't believe this." I scrub my eyes. "How is this possible? Does Sadie know?"

"She knows. So does Charlotte, the human female you call Charlie."

The screen shows the wolves running over a snowy field.

"This is nuts. I can't believe this."

Then the video cuts again, and there's the back of Charlie's house. The big white and gray wolf runs up to the door. It shakes a few times, flinging snow off its thick fur, and scratches the door. The door opens, and there stands Charlie, light streaming behind her, her hand on her belly. She lets the giant wolf in.

"It's not possible." I rub my temples. I feel a little woozy.

"It is possible. It is real." Gabriel lowers himself to the seat beside me. His hand rubs my back. It feels good, soothing. Grounding. "My friend's boyfriends are wolves."

"The preferred term is *wolf shifter*."

"Sure. Okay. Wolf shifter." *Whatever.* "And everyone knows? Even Adele."

"Yes. She found out soon after I met her."

"Wait, what?" I drop my hands. "You met Adele?"

"Why yes. She bore the scarf you crafted. I caught your scent on it. I thought that she was my mate until I discovered the source of the delicious scent. It was the work of a moment to separate you from them. And now you are here, and you are mine. My own." He takes my hand, threading his strong fingers between my limp ones. "My mate."

I tug my hand back. "Back the confessional bus up, Buster. I'm not ready for this."

"Tabitha–" He captures my face in strong but gentle hands. "You're upset."

"Thank you, Captain Obvious," I snap back.

"Shhh, little one. This doesn't need to be a struggle. It's not fair that you had to learn this way, but it is time that you enter into our world."

I'm trembling in his grip. "What do you mean *our world?*"

A flash of gold light from his eyes. His pupils slit and narrow. Just for a second but enough to make me gasp.

"You're one of them." I jerk back, but he's cornered me in the crook of the couch arm.

"I am. And deep down you knew that something was different about them. You're too sensitive not to know." His fingers trace light circles over my shoulder. Soothing me. There's that spiced scent of his, sweet and drugging like mulled wine.

"I… this…I don't understand."

"Do you want me to make it better?" he murmurs. "I can make it better."

I swallow. I want to nod. My heart is cracking open, and I don't know why.

His finger traces the line of my jaw. It feels so good, I can't stand it.

I twist away and push off the sofa. "I need to get out of here."

Gabriel doesn't seem upset at all. He unfolds his big body from the couch. Not a black hair on his head is out of place.

"You can run, Tabitha, but I will chase you. I will always find you."

I whirl and start running blindly, grabbing doorknobs and rushing through. When I come to a door with a keypad on it, I turn and keep running. I don't have a plan. I don't have anything. Gabriel knows this place and probably can tell exactly where I'm going.

Sure enough, when I cross the ballroom he's stalking behind me, taking slow measured steps, but somehow gaining on me.

I race across the ballroom and reach the door, but it's locked.

Gabriel's already beside me. He puts his hand on the keypad, and the door unlocks, slowly swinging open.

I stare at him, chest heaving.

"Run," he murmurs, and I do. Down a hall, up a spiral staircase. Every time I look back, every time I look down, he's a few yards behind me, stalking with that slow measured pace. Gold glittering in his eyes and a half-smile on his face.

My kidnapper likes the chase.

"Run, run, little one." His deep voice echoes up the grand staircase. I reach the top and fling myself into another long hall guarded by suits of armor. The hall forks into two. Left or right?

I dash to the left and around the corner, but it dead ends. *Crap. Wrong way.*

I whirl to go back the way I came, but Gabriel's there, unflappably calm. Darkly beautiful. Clearly enjoying himself. He's not threatening, but he is omnipresent.

I'm committed now.

I try the closest door and end up in a cold shaft that hosts a stone spiral staircase. Up, up, up the stone tower. I'm going in the wrong direction. I need to go down and find a door out of this place. I'm going to end up on the roof of this castle with nowhere to go.

I dash up the stone steps, my footsteps thudding in time to Gabriel's vow. "You will not escape me again."

Gabriel's herding me somewhere. He planned this. I'm at the top of the tower; right where he wants me.

I reach the top step and stagger forward. There's a huge wooden door with a black keypad beside it.

Damn. This is the end. I could pound on the door, but there's no one to answer. No one but me and my handsome kidnapper, stalking me up the stairs.

I sag against the polished wood, resigned to my fate. My forehead rests against the door, my heaving chest brushing it.

I don't even hear Gabriel behind me before his huge body covers mine. "Got you," he murmurs in my ear. His big hand splays across my midriff. At his touch, my heartbeat slows. The hair in the back of my neck raises, but somehow my body has translated all this fear and adrenaline into arousal.

"You're welcome to run anytime you like, Tabitha. I enjoy playing this game. You can run and make me chase, as long as in the end, you know you are mine."

I jerk in his hold, but he's got me wedged between the wall and his large body.

"Still fighting me. Maybe you need some incentive to stay." His lips brush the shell of my ear.

I whimper because it feels so sensual. So delicious.

His hand slips lower, slowly, as if he's waiting to see how I'll react. I should push him away. I consider it—I do. But everything in my body seems to want this. I'm melting back into him, drugged by his delicious scent, the sexy rumble of his voice, his intense focus all on me.

He cups my sex over the thin fabric of my peasant skirt. It's a light touch, undemanding. More of an offer than a violation.

My nipples pebble up. My body relaxes more against his, my tension swirling into an agonized coil in my sex.

I should have stopped to put on a suit of armor if I didn't want him touching me like this. It's dangerous not because he's big and can overpower me with one hand but because his touch feels good, and I like it.

He lightly traces his fingertips over my outer lips, suggesting the pleasure he might give me.

I whimper as my hips lift into his touch.

"Is this what you need, Tabitha? A little reward?" He waits for my answer.

"M-maybe."

"Tell me what pleases you." He slides his hand under my skirt. His fingers play with a satin edge of my panties.

Then he breaches the boundary, dipping his hand between my panties to glide over bare skin until he's cupping me again, the heel of his palm grinding lightly over my clit.

"Mmm," I respond. I can't help myself. I'm lost in sensation and the promise of pleasure.

"So wet." His voice is sin in my ear. "Your body recognizes its master. I can give you what you need."

A sudden pulse of pleasure between my legs almost brings me to my knees. I lean back into his embrace, needing him to keep me upright.

His fingers dip into my sex, making my breath catch.

Everything in my being focuses on the swirl of his strong fingers as he strokes between my labial folds.

There it is! My body strains toward climax. I claw at his arm not to escape, but to make him give me what I want.

"Shhhhh, little one. You don't need to fight." He shifts his weight, pinning me against the door. I'm helpless, unable to move as his finger teases my clit. "You can have what you want. I know what you need. Let me give it to you."

I whimper and rock my hips, seeking more contact with the rough pad of his finger.

"There, that's it," he rasps. I could come from his voice alone. "Take your pleasure. This is your right as my mate."

At the word *mate*, the coil of arousal snaps. Pleasure whips through me. My core tightens, and shivers rush down my inner thighs, straight to the arches of my feet.

"Yes," I gasp, shaking between Gabriel and the wall.

Before the aftershocks stop reverberating through me, he swings me up in his arms. Somehow he frees a hand to open the door. It swings open before him, and he strides into a round room.

The decor and layout are much like the room I woke up in, except we're in a circular tower. The wind whistles outside, but this bedroom is snug and warm, a fire already laid. The black onyx fireplace is shaped like the mouth of a giant dragon. Flames dance between its fangs.

The four-poster bed is bigger than the standard king, made of polished black wood with silk curtains gathered at each corner. The curtains are black with a pattern in gold, the same pattern I saw downstairs—triangles made of three interlooping rings.

Gabriel lays me down on the satin coverlet and draws off my boots. I let him undress me. I'm limp, racked with pleasure. My orgasm was enough to leave my legs like jelly, but my sex is still throbbing. My body misses Gabriel's touch.

Gabriel opens a carved wooden box sitting on the bedside table with one hand. With the other, he gathers my wrists and snaps something into place.

"What the—?" I raise my hands, blinking at the cuffs around my wrists. Twin-wide bracelets of polished gold.

He snaps a second pair onto my ankles before I think to fight.

"Gabriel—"

"Shhhh. Relax. I'm going to give you what you want." He opens a panel beside the bed and keys something in. "I'm going to give you what you need."

There's a beep and some sort of metal strips come flying out of the bedposts. They attach to the cuffs on my wrists and ankle. I tug, but can't get free. I'm bound to the bed by the cuffs and the robotic rope. The cuffs aren't gold, but some sort of magnetic alloy strong enough to tie me down. Is that even possible?

"Do you like them?" Gabriel asks as I examine my bonds. "The design is of my own making. My old world knowledge combined with the new."

"No!" I'm not sure if it's a lie or a truth. My body quivers, a live wire, but I'm pissed. I stare at the sinfully handsome man watching me with that air of faint amusement. "What are you going to do to me?" Instead of sounding scared, my voice comes out breathless, sexy.

Again, my body's completed that peculiar alchemy, turning my fear into arousal. I am splayed out on this giant bed like a virgin sacrifice on an altar. Gabriel has removed his suit jacket and hung it on a nearby chair. Still not a hair out of place.

"Calm yourself, Tabitha. Whatever I do to you, I promise you will like it."

I tug at the cuffs. "I don't like this."

"Lies." His whisper turns soft and sibilant. "I can smell your arousal from here."

I try to press my legs together, but I can't because of the tight bonds.

He chuckles, and damn if the sound doesn't make me even wetter.

Then he raises a skinning knife.

I gasp and twist.

"Hold still," he orders, and the robotic arms tethering me down tighten. My arms are taut in a spread eagle, my body bared to whatever he's going to do.

With swift, decisive moves that look practiced, he slices off my clothes with the wickedly curved blade.

My skirt and my blouse flutter into pieces that he tosses away.

He rests a knee on the bed between my legs. "It's time I tasted my bride."

"Bride?" I gasp over my pounding heart. "I don't remember you proposing marriage."

He chuckles. "This is the way for my kind." He caresses my bare calf above the cuff. "We find the female that belongs to us, and we take her into our keeping. I've shown you my castle. Soon I will show you my lands, my armies. All my treasures. You'll be in awe at what I can give you."

"So I'm supposed to be impressed because you're rich?" I scoff, even as my breath hitches from his hand sliding up my leg. "That's not going to work. My mother's been trying that for years."

"There are other ways of persuading you." He sets down the knife and rolls up his sleeves. Damn if the sight of his forearms isn't the hottest thing I've ever seen. I thought invoking my mother would dampen the flames of my arousal but nope.

I squirm, wriggling as best I can even though I can barely move. "So you're just going to fuck me like this?" I angle my head to glare at the cuff on my right arm then at him.

"No." He's still slowly rolling up his sleeves. "Not tonight. Not even if you beg. Not even if I want to. You'll have to wait for that pleasure."

"Good," I reply, which isn't as eloquent as I'd like. His proximity and smoky scent is doing things to me. All my thoughts are flying out of my head.

He leans over me. "First I'm going to examine you. Then I'm going to worship you as you deserve."

He trails the knife down my shoulder. A flick of his wrist, and he's cut the strap of my bra. Another flick, and he's bared both my breasts. My panties are next to go.

He raises his head and sniffs the air. His eyes flash gold. "Exquisite."

I squirm a little, knowing he's scenting my sex. He stills me with a firm hand on either thigh.

"I'll drink your essence from the source," he vows.

Oh, God. Mini orgasm.

A dark smile slants across his face. "As you will do with mine.""

"Keep dreaming," I bluster, but my eyes flick to the impressive bulge in his black slacks. He's super well-endowed. My inner muscles clench down on air.

He probes me with the knife butt, sliding the smooth handle up and down in a vertical line between my labia lips. Over and over until my hips are rocking.

I whimper when he takes the knife away. With a growl, he lies on the bed with his face at the apex of my legs. His hands slide under my buttocks, lifting me. He kisses my left, then right thigh, his dark hair tickling the sensitive skin. And then he tastes me.

I'll drink your essence from the source.

With my hips lifted, my only view is of the tanned plane of my midriff and the shock of his raven black hair. I can't see what's going on. I can only feel. Gabriel's fingers splay my labia lips, holding me open to his questing tongue. My flesh is swollen and wet from his earlier fingering and my orgasm against the door. This time, when I come, my core clenches, and I try to jacknife off the bed. But I can't move because I'm tied down.

The orgasm wracks my body. Pleasure is a cruel master, straining my already overworked muscles. But still Gabriel's mouth works over my sex, licking, swirling, sucking me down.

Already my orgasm is rising again. I thrash my head back and forth as if I can deny it.

"Gabriel," I plead.

He sits up, his lips wet with my essence. He licks them, and the sight sends another shudder through me. His fingers never leave my body. They twist and probe, circling my clit until my arousal spirals higher.

The pad of his thumb slides down my perineum to press against my rear hole.

My eyes widen. "Gabriel," I warn.

It's no use. He makes me come again with his thumb stroking my rear entrance, stimulating the dark nerves. It's a fuller, more whole sort of pleasure. I hate it. I hate that it feels good.

"Stop." I sigh when his fingers keep moving. His face is in shadow, but I know his gaze is locked on my face. My body is floating off the bed. Endorphins have eclipsed gravity's hold on me. Only the metal ties keep me to earth.

"A few more, *tesoro mio.*"

I jerk my foot. I would kick him if I weren't cuffed. "But what about you?"

His head tips back, lips parting as if he'd drink my scent from the air. "Ah, yes."

He rises up on his knees. He's still fully clothed, unmussed and unwrinkled. I'm a slick and sweaty mess. How does he look so perfect?

If I got free at this moment, the first thing I'd do would grab his head and muss up his hair.

Gabriel opens his slacks enough to take out the proud length of his cock. My eyes snap to it: hard and angry, pre-cum glistening on the tip.

He fists his erection and strokes one giant hand up and down. His eyes lock on mine. He bares his teeth. His strokes quicken. I watch, far more fascinated than I want to be. His breath quickens, and a muscle jumps at his jaw. He stops his breath, and then cum splashes over my bare midriff.

Gabriel growls a word in that guttural language of his. I can guess what it means. *Mine.*

At this point, I'm too overcome to debate it. The robot arms slacken, but I'm too wrung out to move.

He stretches out beside me, and he pulls me into his arms. I typically hate cuddling; it's so awkward, and my partner and I never fit.

But Gabriel and I fit together perfectly. I'm tall and gangly for a woman, but his big body curls around mine. My ass is cradled by his hips. I'm naked, and he's still clothed. Tomorrow, I'll mess up his hair. I'm too tired now.

His head presses into my hair. His lips find my bare neck. "You're my perfect treasure."

"I'm not yours," I mutter.

"But you are, little one. I have claimed you. And soon you will admit it."

I yawn. "I won't," I say sleepily, but I can't deny I'm about to fall asleep in my kidnapper's arms, and it feels amazing.

~

Gabriel

I am a man who enjoys games. Cat and mouse. Hide and seek. Run and chase.

The hunter in me loves to amuse himself this way, and I usually care not whether my opponent enjoys the game or not. But with Tabitha, I'm conflicted.

Is she playing with me?

She allowed me to pleasure her, and I know she enjoyed it. Yet I also believe her protests are genuine. That she's not playing a game to string me along, to make me prove myself.

Yet she doesn't fight, nor does she seem afraid.

She asked about my pleasure. She wanted me to take mine with her.

That's the piece I turn over and over in my head as my beautiful little human slumbers beside me.

What does it mean? Is she simply a generous, giving female? Or does she feel something for me? How far does the mating instinct go in a human? On some level, she must recognize she belongs to me, but perhaps that level is embedded in the vessel, in her body. Her mind rebels against this attachment.

But no, she asked about my pleasure.

This is the loop I continue around until Tabitha falls into a deep sleep, and I quietly get out of bed and put on a robe. I scoop her into my arms with the blankets still around her soft, fragile form, and carry her back to her chamber.

I want to keep her with me in my tower—fate knows how much—but I don't trust myself with her. My usual control slips when she's close.

Frightening her now would be the worst move I could make. I don't trust my dragon not to accidentally harm her. Better to play it safe until we've both had time to get used to each other.

4

Rafe

THE BRIGHT SUN bounces off the hard-crusted snow as I tromp up the pedestrian-only alleys between the shops of Taos. My destination is a cheerfully lit shop with a freshly painted door. I kick the frozen mud from my boots and reach for the gold latch. The bell over the door jingles and the warm scent of chocolate and coffee and caramel and all sorts of delicious things set my mouth watering.

Adele's chocolate shop is her second favorite place on earth. The first is my bed, and I spend long blissful hours each night making sure it remains that way.

I step back to allow two female customers bundled up in hats and scarves to exit. They're carrying white bakery bags filled to the brim with gold boxes of truffles, and they have big smiles on their faces.

When I step inside The Chocolatier, the heat hits my face along with the most delicious scent in the world. No amount of chocolate can compare to the scent of my mate.

It's a little peppery today, a pinch of cayenne mixed into the sweetness. She's worried about something.

When she sees me, her big green eyes round. She starts around the counter. I meet her halfway, plucking her off the floor and setting her on the countertop. I plant my hands on the counter, on either side of her hips and lean in to claim her lips.

My beard scratches against her soft skin.

"Rafe," she sighs against my lips. "You can't. The customers."

"There's no one in the shop." I finger the hem of her wool skirt. "Are you wearing a garter belt today?"

She slaps my hand. "You're not going to find out. Not here."

I grip her hips to keep her from scooting off the counter and escaping. "We'll see about that.

The bell above the door jingles. "Go away." I bark without taking my eyes off Adele. "We're closed."

There's a laugh. "I'll leave these packages outside then."

"Rafe," Adele wriggles in my hold. "I can't believe you. That could've been a customer!"

"I knew it was the mailman. I recognized his scent." I nuzzle the hinge of her jaw where she dabbed a little lavender oil there this morning in lieu of perfume. I dig my fingers into her wealth of curls and hold her still, so I can taste the sensitive spot.

At the touch of my tongue, she gasps. "I need to make rent."

I move so my big body blocks any view of us through the front windows. I kiss along her shoulder. She's wearing a sexy little one of her blouses and a sexy tight skirt. It takes too long to slide her out of the skirt. Easier just to rip it. Even if I face her wrath later.

"I'm sure your landlord will work something out with you."

"That's not what I want." She smacks my arm. I lick over the line of her collarbone.

She grabs my head and forces it back, and I let her. "This is inappropriate workplace behavior," she intones, trying to sound stern even as her lips twitch.

I lean back. "Baby, that's the point."

She rolls her eyes.

"I thought we could have lunch today," I say. "I might be busy with work for the rest of the week."

She hops down and flips the front door sign to "closed for lunch" herself.

I grin at her eagerness. We often eat lunch together. And by "eat lunch together," I mean I feed her and then lay her down on the desk in the tiny room she calls an office and eat her pussy until her curls are mussed, and she's half-drunk on endorphins.

"Are you going on a mission?" she asks.

"No, it's a local gig. Security for some company. Why?"

She nibbles her bottom lip. "I'm worried about Tabitha. She hasn't answered her phone. It's not unusual, but I thought she'd call on Christmas, and we still haven't heard from her."

"She was traveling alone, right?" I could kick myself. We should have put a tracker on her car.

"She's a free spirit. She does sometimes go off the grid for periods, but I just have a funny feeling about it this time."

Adele's fear hits my senses with an icy blast. "Okay, beautiful. I'll get the guys looking for her stat." I pull out my phone and tap a message to Channing right away. As I text, I tell Adele, "We'll see if we can ping her phone and location first. Once we find her, we'll drop a visit to make sure she's okay."

Message sent, I tuck my phone back into my pocket. "We'll find her," I promise, soothing a hand down her back until her fear dissipates in a cloud of lavender.

"Thank you." She leans in and waggles her brows. "Now show me what exactly you want for lunch. Whatever you're craving, I'm sure I can oblige."

∽

Tabitha

I'M in a dark echoing space filled with a warm and smoky scent.

My foot skids on something like gravel. Smooth and clinking. I reach out to steady myself and touch a wall of heated stone.

There's a glow up ahead. I inch along the wall, sliding my hand over the heated wall tiles. I'm in a cloud of a smoky scent, spiced like incense. I'm wearing the blouse and skirt that no longer exists outside this dream—the outfit Gabriel cut off.

My footing slips on the piles of stones. The gravel underfoot is round and clinking like...coins. With one hand still against the wall, I reach down and touch the coins. I sift a few between my fingers, sniffing their metallic scent. My next handful contains a few smooth baubles, smooth like polished stones. Precious gems?

The wall...moves. The glow floods the space, illuminating the gold and jewels glittering at my feet.

I'm face to face with a scaled head. Dark eyes as big as my head glitter like cut diamonds. Smoke curls from the creature's nostrils. The gray plumes eddy around me.

I would fall, but the scaled body of the dragon is coiled behind me, propping me up.

But I'm not scared. This is, after all, a dream.

"What is this place?" I don't speak aloud because in a dream there is no speaking out loud. Communication is silent, my words leaving my head as soon as I think them.

Mine. Treasure. *The dragon speaks mind to mind. I understand perfectly.*

I stoop and collect another gold coin. This one is huge and heavy, ancient.

Yours, *the dragon tells me.* Mate.

Of course. It all makes sense. I'm comfortable and satisfied, resting with the dragon in its dark lair.

The smoky, spicy scent is intenser now. It's like the concentrated scent that emanates from Gabriel's skin. It's not cologne like I first thought it was. But if we could bottle it, we'd make a fortune. Pure, liquid desire.

The dragon lifts its head, turns it, and blows fire. Flames light the room, and when the dragon lowers its head again, a huge hanging lamp overhead remains lit. Shadows dance across the dragon and the cavernous space. Mountains of coins are piled around us, some several stories high. Each mound is studded with multicolored jewels. Emeralds and rubies blink red and green, like Christmas lights on a gold coin tree.

The dragon's scales are red and gold, the color of flickering flames. A scaled foot planted beside me has a glimmering gold cuff banding it.

Oh no. *I point to the dragon's claw.* He has you cuffed, too. *I lift my wrist to show the dragon my cuffs, but in my dream my wrists are bare. I'm free.*

The dragon's rumble shakes the mountains of treasure. A few coins tumble down, threatening an avalanche.

Easy. *I waver as the cave shudders with a dragon-made earthquake. Smoke curls around my ankles. The beast blows out a breath that blasts my skirt back.*

I'm sorry, buddy. *I reach out and touch the scaled head. Reptiles are cold-blooded and dragons are too, but the scales are warm to my touch. The dragon has hidden fires stoked in its belly.*

It's okay, dragon friend. We're in this together now.

The dragon blinks. And then...

I'm sitting on a windowsill in the tower, my legs dangling over the castle wall. I'm not afraid of falling.

I'm no longer wearing the peasant skirt—the one that Gabriel sliced up before he tortured me with orgasms. I'm in a soft pair of joggers that billow a little bit like harem pants.

I lower myself onto a waiting ledge. I don't need to look; I know it'll be there for me. I'm on a stone parapet, a ledge between an inner and outer wall of the castle. The parapet continues along a rampart in a long, gentle decline all the way to the ground. In ancient times, the parapet was a place where soldiers could drop things on the heads of the enemy in a siege. For me, it's an escape route.

The wind whips my hair, tugging at the billowing folds of the harem pants. I walk along the castle wall, my hand skimming the merlons, sticking like jagged teeth from the outer wall. Just beyond the battlement is blue sky. In places, the lip of the outer wall has worn away, and there's nothing between me and a sheer drop down several stories to a cliff face. But I feel pretty confident in the wideness of the ledge. Beyond the castle walls, the rampart is a steep, sloping path to the ground. I walk like a gymnast on a balance beam. There are some patches that are icy but my feet and steps are sure.

The path leads straight down into the mouth of a cave. Smoke drifts from the dark maw of the cave in silver plumes. Like Aladdin's cave of wonders.

The dragon is waiting there. Its red and gold scales shimmer in the light. At times the scales reflect only the blue sky or stone, a camouflage that makes parts of him go invisible.

Thank you, *I tell the dragon. I turn and hike back up the way I came until I reach the open window and climb through into the castle. To my right is a suit of armor. Underneath the open window is a bench. I drop onto it.*

ALPHA'S FIRE

～

When I open my eyes, I'm back in my bedroom—the room I was in the first time I woke up in a castle. I'm in the bed alone. Gabriel didn't spend the night with me, but my body is sore from the pleasure he gave me.

I stretch my arms over the covers. Gold cuffs glint on my wrists. Gabriel kept me cuffed just like the dragon in my dream. *My dream...*

I gasp. It's so obvious. *How did I not understand it last night?*

Gabriel is not a wolf shifter, which I had assumed last night when he told me about Rafe and Deke and Lance.

Gabriel is the dragon!

There are dragons all over this place—how did I not put it together? I think about his strange eyes—the way the pupils change to vertical slits. I'd thought it was a trick of the light, but now I understand what I saw.

My mind races back to our first meeting all those years ago. The water had been steaming hot, yet there were no known hot springs in the area. And then the wind storm… Could it have been kicked up by his wings?

My dream is still with me, complete as a recent memory. It wasn't just a dream. It was a vision. I haven't had one in a long time.

I used to have visions regularly when I was a kid. I'd blurt out what I was seeing without thinking. Until the day I asked my mom's best friend why her husband liked to hug so many women without his clothes on.

She started crying. "I knew he was cheating on me!"

My mom was upset. After her friend left, I had to listen for hours to how uncomfortable I make people, how rude it is to look into their lives and minds without their permission. I was grounded all weekend and missed my friend's birthday party.

That's when I learned to keep my mouth shut about my visions. I couldn't stop them from coming, but I ignored them. Eventually, I stopped having them so often.

Seeing people's auras, being sensitive to their energy is exhausting. That's why I don't hold down jobs for long. No matter how excited I am by a work environment when I start, the energy of everyone rubbing against each other tends to suffocate me. The petty squabbles, the turf wars, the annoyances, the resentments build up until they overwhelm me.

That's why I need to get away from even my closest friends on a regular basis. I need to be alone in wide-open spaces, so I can let my energy expand. I usually keep it tucked in tight.

This space is different. There's a relaxing emptiness to the castle. My energy fills the long, echoing halls. The knot in my chest releases, like I'm able to exhale after years of holding my breath.

Then it hits me. I'm the maiden from the stories. The one the dragon snatches and carries back to his lair. The one the knights try to save with their pitiful swords that are no match for the mighty fire-breathing dragon.

Gabriel brought me here, and he has no intention of letting me leave.

He thinks I'm his mate.

While he doesn't strike me as insane, I'm also certain he's operating from a different set of rules than the ones I live by. You know, like giving a woman her own free will. Not flying her across the sea to a castle in Transylvania as a method of courtship.

Then again, there are other methods of his style of courtship I didn't mind so much last night…

I roll out from under the covers and notice there's an outfit laid on the bed. A crop top and a pair of loose pants. Being a modern woman who prefers to dress herself, I leave the outfit and pick out one of my own from the wonderful closets. I have to admit, he did a good job shopping for me. Everything is my size and to my taste. He certainly put in the effort. I choose a slouchy plum sweater with a neckline that hangs open over one shoulder and a pair of expensive, butter-soft leggings.

I head to the bathroom and clean myself up, finding everything I could possibly need there–brush, skincare, makeup, toothpaste, and floss. I run a brush through my hair.

I'm ready with a hairpin to pick the lock but the massive bedroom door swings open to my touch. I step out into the hallway. I need to get the lay of the castle. More importantly, I need to get my hands on a phone, so I can call Rafe to come and rescue me.

I start one way down the hall then change my mind and turn back, only to gasp.

The tall, thin and painfully proper form of Buttons stands at the end of the hallway.

"Are you looking for something, ma'am?"

"No," I sound breathless, so I square my shoulders and huff. "No," I return with a lot more aplomb. My stomach growls so loud we both startle.

Perfect timing. "Actually, breakfast would be good." I can blame my wanderlust on my hunger.

"Yes, of course," he says. "I was coming to fetch you."

"Okay." Interesting.

"Where is Gabriel?"

"Master Dieter had some business that required his attention, but he said to tell you he will join you for lunch."

Oh for heaven's sake. Are we pretending I'm not a prisoner here?

I test it. "Before breakfast, can you provide me with a phone? I need to get in touch with my mother. She will be worried about me."

Buttons has the grace to look chagrined. "I'm afraid you will have to speak to Master Dieter about that matter."

Right. That's what I thought.

"After breakfast, I thought I would also show you the library since the Master told me that you enjoyed it."

Okay, I'll play the game. "That sounds nice."

When I glance over, the aura around his spare frame glows a welcoming pink and purple. Sunset colors. Buttons can't be evil. People I've met who aren't kind people have muddy auras with blacks and browns and grays. Sometimes there's red around their heads signaling anger. Buttons' aura shows a person with a big heart.

"Would you prefer to eat in your room or the dining room?"

"Not my room," I say quickly. I don't think it's irrational that I'm nervous about getting locked up in there.

"Very well." He sweeps out a hand. "Shall we?"

He navigates the maze halls easily and leads me to an elevator.

"Is your name really Buttons?" I ask.

"Yes," he says. "It is the curse of all the Buttons to sound like we are children's book characters."

I look to the side to hide a grin. Maybe if I get to know him a little better, I can ask to use his first name.

The door opens, and he waits for me to exit first. Ahead is the grand dining hall, with the long table and one lonely chair. I hesitate.

"Is something wrong, madam?"

"I want to eat here, but the dining room is so formal."

Buttons gives a small smile and presses a button, so the elevator door closes. The colors of his aura warm even more. "I understand, and I know just the place where you might be more comfortable."

The elevator descends another floor and opens at the foot of a plain staircase and hallway that would fit into an ordinary house. None of the red carpet and gilt-framed wall paneling of the grand rooms upstairs. This is an Upstairs/Downstairs moment unless Mr Buttons is actually a serial killer, and his cutesy name covers up his maniacal tendencies.

I take a breath to steady myself as I precede Buttons out of the elevator. Strains of opera music float up the hall. Someone is singing along in a reedy voice that's slightly off-tune.

I give Buttons a curious glance, and he tilts his head for me to keep walking. He's got a fond look on his face.

The end of the hall widens to a large, arched doorway. Light spills over our feet, and the scent of rising bread hits me.

"*Ooh.*" I glide forward into the warm space. The room has a stone floor and massive butcher block island. Even the huge stainless steel appliances don't detract from its old-world charm. Colorful tile mosaic on the walls. The space could fit a dozen people but still feels cute and cozy. There are bouquets of flowers in colorful Polish pottery vases that match the tiles on the wall. The pattern is blue and white with some red and yellow thrown in.

A petite man with corkscrew brown curls springing out from under his big white chef's hat is leaning over an oven. He's the one singing along with Pavarotti. His voice rises to a crescendo.

The chef's aura is sparkling yellow with touches of pink. Buttons watches him almost fondly, an expression so far from his usual prim and proper look, it gives me whiplash.

When the music dies away, Buttons clears his throat.

The shorter man whirls around, his curls flying this way and that. A stream of Italian flows from his mouth. I only catch a few words– *mio cuore, my heart,* and *non dovresti, you should not.*

"Chef Giampi," Buttons says in a voice a few degrees more relaxed than his usual stuffy tone. "May I present to you, Miss–"

"Please just call me Tabitha," I interrupt.

"Ah yes," Chep Giampi looks at me like I'm his long-lost sister. He runs over, sketches a bow, grabs my hand, and kisses it. "It is a pleasure to meet you. What brings you to my kitchen today?"

My stomach enters the conversation, gurgling loud enough to rival the opening strains of *Nessun dorma*. Chef Giampi runs to press a floury finger to the music system. The music volume cuts down to a barely audible hum.

"*La colazione?*" The chef opens the oven and a yeasty blend of baking dough and cinnamon sugar hits me. My stomach roars.

"Yes," Buttons guides me to a stool at the island. "The lady is hungry. I'll make tea."

Giampi rushes around, flinging dish towels and opening and closing cupboards. Buttons works more methodically, opening a fridge and setting a bowl of fresh figs in front of me.

"Start with these," he says and busies himself with a red tea kettle.

I grab a fig and pop it into my mouth to silence the beast in my belly, but then I feel rude. "I don't want to intrude. If it's too much trouble–"

"No, is no trouble!" Giampi shouts. He's at the other

end of the butcher block, half disappeared in a cloud of flour. "I make you *sfogliatella*, the way my nonna told me. You will think you have been kissed by an angel."

Sfogliatelle is a lobster claw, a decadent pastry filled with cream. "I really don't need…"

"Allow him to bake for you," Buttons advises. He sets down a full tea service: a little pitcher of milk, a bowl of sugar, a sturdy tea mug with a matching saucer. All the pottery has the same print as the vases and walls. "The pastry will not go to waste. There are plenty of soldiers here to eat them."

"Soldiers?"

"Oh yes. Master Dieter has generously allowed the staff a month off for the holidays, but his mercenary types are still here." He sniffs like he doesn't approve.

Mercenary types? Maybe that's who I heard when I was trying to escape. Soldiers patrolling.

"Really?"

"Yes. Perhaps you've seen them training in the courtyard?"

"Um, no. I haven't really gotten out of my room that much…"

"That is why I was coming to fetch you. No reason for you to be cooped up, unless you decide you want to rest."

"Oh no, I'm rested enough."

"Then this is just what you need. We enjoy the company."

"Thank you. I didn't really want to eat alone in the dining room. I mean who does that?" I wrinkle my nose.

"*Il Senore* prefers to eat *solo*," Giampi says.

"*Il Senore* being Master Dieter," Buttons says. The two of them weave around each other in a practiced dance. When they're close to each other, both their auras change to pink and blend together seamlessly. Pink is heart chakra energy. Love.

I need to stop staring. "Well, I'm not him," I say, unfolding the napkin Buttons placed by my side, along with a place and cutlery. "Where is he anyway?"

"He is in his office. He had some business to attend to," Buttons says. "He has holdings all over the world."

"Really?" Maybe I can get these two lovely people to tell me more about my captor's habits. I can figure out how I can use them against him and escape. "Please tell me more." I prop my chin on my hand. "I want to know everything."

~

Gabriel

Being away from Tabitha all morning is torture, yet I tell myself it's what she needs. I can't smother or overwhelm her. She will require time and space to get used to her new surroundings. Her new life with me.

I note her location on my phone when I come out of my meeting via the trackers installed in her wrist cuffs. Huh. She's in the kitchen.

That's a strange place for the lady of the castle to be. I mean, I don't require her to manage the kitchen, it is beautifully managed by my chef and Buttons. Even though there's no reason to suspect something's gone wrong, I find my step quickening as I make my way to the castle kitchen.

There, I'm surprised by what I find.

My bride, sitting at the large wooden block table with both my butler and my chef.

I clear my throat, and both Buttons and Giampi jump to their feet.

"Master Dieter, you have returned," Buttons says.

"I have." My gaze is on Tabitha, who has twisted in her seat to look my way. Her face is full of light. She's more relaxed than I've seen her since she arrived, and there's a lovely smile in place, which droops slightly when she sees me. Maybe because I'm frowning.

That's not like me. I usually don't allow emotions to show on my face. I usually don't feel emotions. "Why are you eating in the kitchen?" I ask.

She waves a dismissive hand at me. "Your dining room is far too formal. I prefer it here."

She prefers it…with my servants?

I try to dislodge the jealous bone that gets stuck in my throat. Surely she's not interested in either man. They are a couple. They don't seek the attention of women.

My brain reels trying to figure out what they could have offered her to make her smile that my dining room and I didn't.

I force a smooth demeanor back in place. "I see. Will you join me in the library?"

To my relief, she stands. "Yes. We have some things to discuss," she says.

"Whatever you like, my treasure," I say, taking her hand when she approaches. She withdraws it, and I shift to placing my hand at her lower back, guiding her out to the hallway and in the direction of the library.

"What I would like is to leave," she says primly, and my heart shoots down to my feet.

"I'm afraid that is not a possibility, my treasure," I say smoothly. I have to squelch the blast of heat from my dragon's internal fire that threatens to erupt.

"You can't keep me as your prisoner here."

"Tabitha, you are not my prisoner. You are my mate. Queen of this castle. Born to rule at my side."

"News flash, I'm not some fair maiden you can carry

off and keep in your tower. My knights will come to rescue me."

Steam comes out of my nostrils, and I avert my head to keep her from seeing. "Are you referring to your wolves?" I ask when I'm back in control.

"Yes."

"I'm sure they will try, but they will not succeed." Gah. This is not how I wished our conversation to go. Not at all. I don't want Tabitha to feel like a prisoner. But there's no way I can let her leave. A dragon never relinquishes his treasure. Especially not a mate. And keeping her safe consumes me enough, even with her here protected in my castle.

I lost a mate once.

I won't lose her again.

She lifts her lovely chin. "I know what you are."

"Ah. I wondered when you would figure it out. Did Buttons tell you?"

We arrive at the library, and I lead her to a seat in front of the fire, watching with pleasure at how graceful and glorious she looks when she curls up in the overstuffed chair, her legs tucked up to the side, her hair falling over her bare shoulder. She's truly magnificent.

"I had a dream."

I lean forward and pin her with my gaze. "Did you? What did you see?"

She tilts her head and studies me back. "There was a dragon in a cave. He wore gold cuffs like mine." She holds her wrists up.

I draw in a sharp breath through my nose, sensing an angry stirring of my dragon within. Do I keep him in cuffs?

Perhaps I do.

With good reason. When he gets free, he rampages. Especially where our mate is concerned.

Most recently, he torched that drug cartel in New Mexico that had been threatening Adele, who I believed was my mate because she'd been wearing Tabitha's scarf.

"You saw my other form."

She doesn't seem afraid. Not like she was when I picked her up in New Mexico. When she fainted dead at the sight of me. "I saw."

"Did he…speak to you?"

My dragon used to speak to me. His animalistic urges, his desires were in my mind, even when I was in this form. But no longer. Now I only feel his pain. His resentment.

As I'm sure he feels mine.

"Yes. He spoke into my mind."

A lump forms in my throat. I'm both healed and torn apart knowing Tabitha and the dragon side of me have bonded. Torn apart because this side of me still stands so far apart from both of them.

"What did he tell you?"

She hesitates a moment. "He showed me his treasure."

My lips kick up. Of course he did. "Ah, yes. We dragons love our treasure."

"I don't care about your treasure," she says with a note of challenge.

"Yes, I'm coming to see that. But I have other ways of persuading you to stay."

"So you *are* persuading me? Because I'm not feeling like I have much of a choice here."

Malediction. Normally I would have moves and counter-moves all prepared in advance, but with Tabitha, it all feels wrong. *She* feels right. Being with her is completion, but there's no joy in tricking her or trapping her.

She's my mate. I want her to be here willingly.

And yet, letting her go is an absolute impossibility.

"It's only been a day, my treasure. Give us time to settle together. You will come to love me, I'm sure."

Anger flashes in her pale green eyes. "I see."

She is still fighting, but I can be patient. She will come to accept me and my home as her own. Like all brides carried off to new lands, she will come to love her husband and honor him with offspring and her sweet obedience.

"How old are you?" she asks, changing the subject.

"Old. Dragons live a long time."

"Give me a ballpark date."

My brow furrows at the question. I do not know what this ballpark refers to.

"Estimation," she amends. "You need to work on updating your lingo, dragon."

"Which calendar? Gregorian or Julian?"

Tabitha wrinkles her adorable nose, like she's trying to remember her history. "The Julian calendar hasn't been used since the Middle Ages."

I hold her gaze, and she sucks in a breath. "You're telling me you've been around since before the Renaissance?"

"Yes. I may have even participated in it."

She covers her eyes with a hand.

"Tabitha?"

"I need a minute. Talk about a May-December romance. No wonder your ideas are medieval."

I wait silently until she lowers her hand, then I capture it in mine. She looks at our joined hands. This time she doesn't pull away. There's an electrical charge between us, zinging under my skin. She can't fight the attraction between us. The pheromones are too strong.

Her body knows its master.

"You're a relic," she says. "This is why you don't get my pop culture references."

"You can teach me," I offer. "I have a facility with many languages. I can learn the new words you speak of."

"What is the language you spoke last night? After you lay down with me?"

"A dialect long lost to the modern age. The language of dragons."

"Really? Wow."

"Once we are fully mated, you may understand it."

If I can keep my dragon in check enough to safely claim her.

"Seriously? How does that work?"

"You seem quite sensitive. You have psychic abilities, no?"

She blushes, as if it's a flaw, not a gift. "Yes. My mother hated it because she said I embarrassed people by knowing their secrets."

"It's your gift. And a gift to me. It makes you a perfect match for me." I play with her delicate fingers, examining them, marveling at how small they are.

"Your hands are hot, like you have burning coals under your skin."

"The fire is always alive, ready to pour forth when there's danger. It can be dangerous."

I didn't mean to admit that, but she's my mate. My treasure. It could affect her.

"I didn't think dragons were around anymore. Of course, I didn't think werewolves existed either. But there are legends all over the world of dragons. Like St. George slaying the dragon."

"Ah yes, Bruce," I say. "He wasn't too right in the head. He smoked a lot of peat moss. Said it was good for his health."

I grin at Tabitha's astonished expression, and she shakes her head. "You're trolling me."

"Trolling?" Another unfamiliar turn of speech, but this one I can guess at the meaning of. "St. George didn't kill him. Just wounded."

"Really?"

"Yes." I frown. "But I don't know what happened to him. Probably fell into a bog. As the British say, poor sod."

Tabitha snort-laughs. "You really have lived a long time. Next, you'll be telling me about Grendel."

"Don't get me started on him and his mother. Or King *Artur*."

Tabitha's smile is genuine–like the one I saw when she was in the kitchen. Could it be all she craves is *this*?

A bit of conversation?

That was all Buttons and Giampi had given her.

"I need to call my mother," she tells me, lifting her shapely brows.

I anticipated this request, yet it pains me more than I expect to refuse it. I hate to refuse my bride anything. "In due time, Tabitha."

"When?" she presses, undaunted by my refusal.

"After you've settled here."

"Right." She removes her hand from mine and stands. "I'm going to my room. Is that allowed, your royal dragon highness?"

She's peevish, which is understandable.

I stand with her. "Of course, my treasure. I will escort you there."

"*No.*" She holds up a hand, as regal as any castle's queen. "I'll find it myself." With that, she turns on her heel, tosses her lovely locks and strides from the room.

It takes everything in me not to follow her. To snatch her back with an arm around her waist and press her up against the wall. To make her melt with my tongue between her legs as I did last night. I could so easily use her body against her. Show her the connection, the bond we share that can't be denied. Can't be broken.

But I must restrain myself. A tincture of time—that is what this situation requires.

Or so I believed.

5

Tabitha

I slam the door to my bedroom and pace around the length of it. The *nerve* of this guy.

He's nuts.

No, not nuts. He's just truly medieval. He has no idea how insane his way of thinking is in this day and age.

Part of me can't blame him. The part of me that's fascinated by him. Drawn to the devilishly handsome looks and the suave manners. The incredible fact that he is actually a dragon!

On some level, I'm already in love with the dragon I saw in my dream.

But I'm not the sort of woman who can be bought. Nor am I one you can keep in a cage.

My mother may be into both of those scenarios but not me.

And as I sat there listening to his nonsense about me getting used to him and living here, I realized I don't have to wait for Rafe and the guys to find me. Hell, they probably don't even know I'm in trouble yet.

The dragon showed me the way out of the castle in my vision. For the first time in a long time, I'm going to follow my instincts and allow my vision to guide me.

I check the window above the tub, but it's stuck closed. *Not here.* If I angle my head I can almost see that parapet hugging the outer wall of the castle. I can't access it from here, but in my dream, I climbed through a different window. One in the hall, next to a suit of armor.

I grab boots and the warmest coat I can find. I don't mind the cold—my friends tease me about wearing skirts and short sleeves even in the snow—but winter in Romania means freezing temperatures. I add a few more layers—a wool sweater, a long-sleeved shirt. A pair of down ski-weather-worthy joggers over the leggings. Might as well layer up.

I pad down the hall in the sensible walking boots that I chose for my excursion. I round the corner, and my breath catches. There it is—the red carpet, the suit of armor, the bench against the window.

Unlike in my dream, the window is a pain to unlatch and move outward. I'm considering wrenching the arm from the suit of armor and using it to bash open the glass when the window hinge creaks, and it shudders open.

It's easy enough to step on the bench and stick my head out. The wind tugs at my hair. This is a lot scarier than my dream, but there is a ledge I can climb onto. This is it. This is my way out of the castle.

I don't have a phone or my wallet or purse or anything. I'll have to get out and away and find someone who can help me. They might not speak English, but between the few words I know in German and Dutch, and my mediocre Italian, maybe I can get them to understand. At least let me make a phone call.

But I'm getting ahead of myself. First I must escape.

Stepping onto the ledge takes a lot more willpower than it did in my dream. The cold air is a dagger in my lungs. My face freezes in the wind. One gust could pick me up and blow me over the edge. If I were an ancient archer, these working conditions would suck. How in the heck did ancient warriors stand it?

I crouch as I inch down the icy ledge, hugging the side of the castle. My steps are tremulous. I need to be careful. I have a lot more vertigo than I did in my dream.

"This is nuts," I mumble through frozen lips. It's comforting to talk to myself even if the howling wind carries my voice away. "Why am I clinging to the side of the castle on a cold winter day? Oh, you know, the usual. A madman kidnapped me and imprisoned me and gave me too many orgasms to count. Then I dreamed of a dragon and a treasure-filled cave who showed me how to escape!"

I scoot a millimeter to the left, my eyes on the fog in front of me. The castle is so high up, I'm literally in a cloud.

"Too bad he didn't provide a magic carpet to fly me away."

I reach an area where there are no merlons to protect me from the wind or the drop. The parapet is narrower here, too. Parts of it have crumbled away. I get down on my butt and scoot stone by stone.

The gray mist blows past me, revealing snatches of white and brown earth to my right, way, way too far below. I avert my eyes, so I can keep breathing.

"Oh, that's right, dragons don't need a carpet to fly. They have wings."

Even though I'm on my butt, at times I can see into the massive courtyard. There are people in black military-like uniforms down there, looking like ants on the ground. This adds another layer of fun to my icy excursion. And by fun, I mean stress.

My stomach gurgles. Is it still morning? I should've searched for a kitchen to grab some meal bars. My arms are growing weak.

This was so much easier in the dream. I had that strange floaty quality, like I could fly. And the way down was so smooth. Warmer, and the dragon was waiting for me in the cave.

The wind has surged. Now I'm buffeted on all sides. Snowflakes swirl around me, frosting my face. My muscles are stiff. I want to rest, but if I don't keep moving, I'm going to freeze to the stone.

Why did I think this was a good idea?

I pull myself along, inch by inch. The metal cuffs I'm wearing clink against the stone. I can't get them off, dammit. I tried clawing them off, but they're seamlessly welded together around my wrists.

If I can get out of here, I can find someone to get them off.

I need to keep going.

I'm trying to catch my breath when a gust tries to pull me over the side. My shout is swallowed by the whistling wind.

I give in, and I lie down fully, army crawling across the icy stone. Another blast like that could push me off this ledge. If it blew to the left, I'd fall into the courtyard, shattering every bone I have. To the right, and I'll fall not just several stories down a castle wall but another several thousand feet down a rocky cliff.

After what feels like ten hours later and a few fearful slips that take years off my life, the mists part ahead of me to reveal the end of the ledge and castle wall. In my dream I somehow danced down the rampart all the way to the ground. I peek over the low wall. The ground is so far down, clouds drift between me and the snowy ground. *Not going down that way.*

In despair, I crawl forward a little more and come to an open hole. Flecks of snow are falling into the opening, onto the stairs. *A stairwell!*

I'm in some sort of outer keep that's no longer attached to the main, more modernized part of the castle.

I scramble to lower myself down. This wasn't in the dream, but this makes it easy doesn't it?

Voices echo nearby. I freeze, but my foot hits a step, and the stone crumbles underneath.

Maybe not so easy after all.

It takes a year for the voices to move away. Another century for me to peel my aching, freezing, filthy self off one ancient step and lower myself to the next. The only sound is my stifled breathing and the clink of my gold cuffs against the stone. My hands are stiff with the cold.

A cold light leads me to an open door frame. A pristine plume of snow has blown in a few feet. I cup some in my hands and give myself a freezing drink. Keeping out of the wind, I creep to the stone-framed opening and look out.

I did it. I've reached the ground. I'm at the base of the castle. But there's no cave of wonders nor dragon waiting for me outside. Of course, there isn't. It was just a vision. Some kind of metaphor. There's nothing but a huge snow-covered rock where the mouth of the cave was in my dreams, with smaller piles of rocks and snowdrifts around it. A couple hundred feet of boulders and the ground slopes, becoming the sheer face of the mountain. If I'm going to escape, I'm going to have to find a path down the mountain.

I could just sit here and hope a rescue comes, but it's pretty unlikely. My friends won't know I'm missing until they can't get a hold of me for weeks. Meanwhile, Gabriel is video monitoring their home and every move.

I have to escape. To get free and to warn them.

Behind me, a man calls to another, their voices muffled by the wind and stone.

I duck out of the doorway, and the cuffs around my wrists start beeping.

Shit!

I scramble over the boulders. I have to get away or someone's going to hear and start looking for me.

I clamber over the boulders as quickly as I can. Once I'm out of sight of the doorway, I drop down and hug an icy rock. My wrist cuffs have stopped beeping, and no one's shouting as they come after me, but that doesn't mean they won't come.

I try to shift my weight and inch backward. One boulder foothold at a time.

The snow's stopped, and the clouds have cleared, leaving a hazy sun filling the day with anemic light. I can't feel my hands. My pants are heavy with filthy ice. My legs and arms are shaking. Cold sweat plasters all my layers to my clammy skin. The coat and the layers I'm bundled in keep me warm, but the tips of my ears are freezing.

This is nuts. I didn't sign up to free climb down the freaking cliff.

I cling to the weathered stone, scraping my cheek against the rough slate as I look down. Below me are clouds. Below them, the snow-frosted tops of pine trees.

I can't do this. I love rock climbing, but not this much. And not under these conditions.

I close my eyes and try to bring up the feeling of the dream.

Help me, Dragon. You got me into this mess. Show me the way out.

GABRIEL

After my meeting with Tabitha, I was too restless to do anything. The need to claim her, to fill her with my seed and brand her with my tongue consumed me.

I don't like having her here against her will. While she doesn't seem overly stressed or frightened, I know she's not happy with me.

"Bring Tabitha lunch in her room," I instruct Buttons. "She wished to be alone for a while."

So stay the fuck away from her.

I don't say that part because it's not right. I want her to rely on Buttons, to trust him if she cannot trust me.

But that does nothing to stop the billows of steam trailing from my nose.

Buttons gives me an astute look. "Of course, Master Dieter. I will make sure she has everything she needs for a quiet afternoon. Do you require anything?"

"No," I snap.

"Perhaps some fresh air would help. Stretching your… wings a bit?"

A growl rumbles in my throat. My dragon threatening to erupt.

Buttons is right.

I'm losing control, and I can't let that happen. I can't let my dragon take charge. He's way too dangerous.

"I think you're right. I will patrol the boundaries of my land. I must ensure my mate's safety." Stretching my wings will take the edge off, let my dragon out of the cage for a while, so I can keep control.

I don't want to forcibly claim my bride. Nor do I want to rush her.

"She is safe here," he says in a soft voice. Like he's

speaking to my dragon, not me. He must see how close to the surface the dragon is.

How much danger he is in.

A cold shudder runs through me at the idea of ever harming these humans who are here at my service. They wouldn't deserve that fiery fate.

I have to be vigilant. Have to keep myself in control.

I manage to incline my head at Buttons who bows in return, and then I take off swiftly for the castle keep. The moment I hit the fresh air, I break into a run, throwing off my clothes as I go. I shift mid-stride, taking flight the moment my clothes hit the frozen earth. Once I'm in the air, I turn invisible to protect the villagers from my secret. They will only feel the wind whipping off my wings when I fly above them.

The freezing air helps cool my distemper, and I beat my wings to take me higher and higher, soaring into the clouds until I break above them, where the air is thin, but the sun shines.

There I can breathe. I duck my head and pump my wings, glorying in the sensation of wind across my scales, the speed I can move at when I let myself go.

I fly for over an hour, maybe two, until my blood has cooled, and the fires within me are down to glowing embers. Pumping my sore wings, I turn back.

Gabriel! I hear Tabitha. Or I sense her. She's speaking to me, in my mind.

Oh, fates.

She's calling for help.

~

Tabitha

My cuff beeps in my ear, and I startle.

The rock under my foot gives way, and I slide a foot or two before my feet find a ledge. I cement my trembling body to the rough rock face, my scream cutting off when I lose my breath. My cuffs are beeping like crazy again, drowning out the thud of my pounding heart.

A shadow glides over the rock face I instinctively hunch, pressing my scraped face and hands to become one with the cliff.

A blast of wind buffets my legs. Smoke plumes above my head. There's something behind me, its hot breath surrounding me.

Inch by inch, I twist my head around. And there he is: the dragon from my dream, the sun, and sky glinting off of red gold scales.

Magnificent. Beautiful. Furious.

The huge wings beat the air in a lazy rhythm. Soft gusts surround me.

"Hi, Gabriel," I say weakly.

Its clawed hand descends. My primal monkey brain can't take it, and I scream.

Then my stomach tumbles to my feet. The world flips and falls away, the ground far below, tilting at dizzying speed. I'm wedged against hard scales. I can't move. The dragon's got his claws around me. I'm safely in his grip, but my legs are cold where they're sticking out from my bunched-up joggers. I angle my head and get a dizzying view of the ground below. It's like peering from the window of a small airplane, except the freezing wind rushes over my face. My scream stabs my ears.

Far, far below is the castle, its walls and turrets the size of a child's toy. I squeeze my eyes shut. The dragon snaps its wings, and we plummet.

I'm still screaming, out loud or in my head or both. I

keep my eyes shut so tight, my forehead throbs. Then I land on a cold, hard, flat surface.

The beeping cuffs on my wrists fall blissfully silent.

With wind blasting from under its wings and whipping through my hair, the dragon lands beside me, in the middle of the castle courtyard. The space I thought was huge now seems just large enough to hold it. The tips of his folded wings reach two stories high. Its wedge-shaped head is as big as a car. Patches of scales shimmer and reflect the sky, effectively turning it invisible.

The dragon can turn invisible. So that's how he crept up on me in the desert after Gabriel lured me to the middle of nowhere. He was invisible.

No sign of the men in uniform I saw before. What does Buttons think of a creature from a medieval myth landing in the castle courtyard? The prim and proper butler probably knows the proper etiquette for welcoming a dragon. Or maybe Gabriel mostly stays invisible.

It tips its mighty head up to the sky and breathes fire into the air–a bellow of rage. The heat warms me, even from a distance.

Gabriel is angry.

Funny how I'm not the least bit afraid of him in this form. I was afraid of falling. Afraid of flying, dangling from his talons. But I'm not frightened of the dragon.

I somehow instinctively know that he will always protect me.

His anger is only that I was in danger.

That I left him.

There's a hum, and my cuffs snap to the ground.

Eek! I'm lying on some sort of metal sheet, and the cuffs are doing that magnet thing again, holding me down. I struggle, but by the time I've freed myself, metal bars have spiraled out of the platform edge surrounding me. I'm in a round prison, a cage with no lid.

"Gabriel," I yell in frustration. "Gabriel!"

Across the courtyard, the dragon stares at me impassively. The entire platform, bars and all, shudders and begins to descend.

6

Gabriel

Once Tabitha is safely underground, I shift back to my human form and yank on a pair of pants.

She nearly died.

My mate nearly died.

It's a fucking wonder the dragon didn't destroy a whole city in his rage. Thank fate we saved her. Our sweet, beautiful, very naughty mate.

I don't want to imprisoner her, but–

Oh, who am I kidding? Some part of me always knew it would come to this. That was why I had the cuff technology developed to track her and trap her. To hold her in any position I like, anywhere I like. And right now, I have her spread eagle on the platform and completely at my mercy. Tabitha is mine, and she's about to find out what happens when she puts her safety at risk.

When she tries to leave me.

Of course, I did encourage her to run that first night in the castle.

That was foolish of me. I never imagined she would risk her neck climbing the edge of a crumbling rock ledge!

Fate, what if she'd fallen? What if I hadn't been in dragon form, at the ready to catch her with my claws? What if I hadn't been at the castle at all?

I would've lost her again. Once more, before I ever claimed her!

Fate may not favor me so much as I believed when my bride first woke me from dragon's slumber.

I don't go to my mate immediately. I'm too angry. Too upset about almost losing her again. Yet I can't stay away, either. I stay in the shadows, needing to be near, letting her scent, the fact that she is still alive, soothe away the rampaging rage that I fear most.

∽

Tabitha

The lower the cage descends, the less the bracelets are magnetized.

I sit up, my palms planted on the cold metal, trying to orient myself. Something closes overhead, cutting off my view of the sky and leaving me in the dark, like I'm in an elevator shaft of some kind. Machines whir. The cage keeps descending.

I grab the bars and take a deep breath. Adrenaline courses through me.

The dragon was incredible. And he can turn invisible.

That's why I don't remember our second meeting. That's why I fainted. He lured me to the desert, and then a dragon appeared, and I passed out from shock.

Machinery hums, and the cage stops. I'm alone in the

cool darkness. At least there's air blowing in from somewhere, and it's fresh and clean.

Slowly, a few lights blink on, and I retreat to the center of my cage. I'm in a huge warehouse-like space. The few fluorescent lights illuminate the far-off walls and the raised platform the cage rests on. A humming sound whirs nearby. Somewhere in here is a server room with an army of fans blowing to keep the place cool.

Even though the air is cool, I'm too hot in the heavy coat and layers. I tug everything but my original outfit off. My hands are warmer now. I flex them to get the blood pumping through them and wipe them on the coat.

With my movement, more lights have cut on, spotlighting the area twenty feet ahead of me—another raised platform with desks and mounted screens. Either an epic gaming setup, or Gabriel is building a superweapon to control the world.

Even though I'm trapped and cuffed in a cage, my sudden giggle echoes around the dark hollow space. "Seriously?" I say out loud because Gabriel must be listening. "You brought me to your evil lair?"

I sit up and grab the bars. "You just need a big fluffy cat that you can pet. Or is that Buttons? Is he a house cat shifter?" My burst of laughter bounces off the walls.

I let loose until I can get a hold of myself. My heartbeat drums under the gold cuffs. If Gabriel doesn't come to me soon, I'm going to lose it and start humming the *Goldfinger* theme song.

"I know you're watching me from somewhere. You might as well come let me out."

Brighter lights cut on, and I flinch. Beyond the large warehouse space is a wide staircase, half of it out of sight because of the low ceiling. Somewhere above them, a door slams.

Gabriel steps down, slowly coming into view, and I lose my breath. I've seen Gabriel wear a suit—no man ever wore a suit so well—but I've never seen him without a shirt. He's wearing black pants, this time loose black joggers that look casual but cost more than my car. His torso is bare, his bronze skin gleaming in the low light.

He prowls forward, his feet bare on the concrete floor. Even with the eerie greeny-white light straight out of a horror movie playing over his face, he's beautiful.

I grip the bars and pull myself up. I'm not cold or tired or hungry anymore. My body is charged with adrenaline.

His incense-like scent surrounds me. I suck in lungfuls of it, and it charges my blood even more.

"You risked your life to get away from me," he chokes.

I'm pressed against the bars now.

"I could have lost you." He stops a few feet away, and there's a hollow in my belly. I'm aching, not being able to touch him.

"You saved me, though."

His eyes light with gold flame. Twin lines of gray smoke trail from his nostrils. Any second now, he's going to belch fire.

"You're the dragon," I murmur in a dreamy tone. Without thinking, I reach for him.

His face is frozen, but he moves closer. I put my hand out and touch his face. He's just too beautiful to be real. Smoke caresses my face.

I cup his cheek. He closes his startling amber and gold eyes and leans into my palm, looking vulnerable. It does something to me.

Changes me, somehow, seeing him this way. Now that I equate him with the dragon that I'm so certain I can trust, I can't bring myself to resent him. Not even when he has me locked up in this cage. He is one and the same as that ancient beast in the cave who wants to show me his treasure and rescue me from every danger.

I can't stop touching him. His skin is warm, heated from inner fires, like the dragon scales in my dream. I mold my hands to the harsh planes of his face, scratching over his beard and around the firm line of his jaw and into his thick hair. I don't have to mess his black hair up, it's already wind-whipped and unruly. I love this look on him.

"You could have been hurt," he rasps against my palm. His eyes are still closed, his dark lashes, long and silky against his bronze skin. "You could've died."

"I know." I'll admit that the second part of my plan was completely stupid.

"The rock climbing bit was a mistake. But the plan worked up until that point."

His sigh gusts across my palm. "How did you even find the way out?"

"I had a dream." Not sure why, but I don't want to mention how his dragon showed me in the vision right now.

"Your gift," he mutters.

My hands have wandered down to his muscles. I can't help it, they're laid out in front of me in a mouth-watering display. My hands look so small against the bunched muscles of his shoulders and the broad planes of his pectorals. If I could find my voice, I'd thank him for coming to me before he bothered to put on a shirt.

When I plant my right hand over his beating heart, his eyes snap open. "Tell me one reason I should let you out of this cage." His pupils are elongating, narrowing to the slits of a snake.

I slide my hand lower, exploring the taut cobblestones of his abs.

"I can think of a few reasons." I hold his gaze as I slip

my hand into his pants. I'm earning my way out of this cage, but it's no hardship–heh–no pun intended. I'm more turned on by Gabriel right now than I ever have been by a man. Something about knowing he's the incredible dragon, knowing he believes I'm his mate, that he belongs to me and I belong to him, makes my body sizzle with sexual excitement.

His joggers are loose and just as expensive-feeling as they look. He pulled them on commando. Lucky me.

Crisp hairs prickle in my palms. His shaft is long and hot, throbbing in my hand. His girth stretches my fingers. My eyes widen.

Gabriel's gaze is wild on mine.

I sense my power here.

Then his expression shutters to hide what he didn't mean to reveal. "On your knees," he orders.

I sink down. Electricity courses through my body, bright and amber-colored. I tug down the joggers. His hands grip the bars over my head. His shaft juts through the cage bars, level with my mouth.

Oh yes. I am going to enjoy this. I lick my lips. If this won't convince him to let me out of the cage, nothing will.

I reach for his cock, and he tsks.

"No. Mouth only."

Gabriel has serious control issues. I let him have his way since he so clearly has the upper hand. I set my hands and forehead on the bars and dart my tongue forward to lick the tip of him, tasting salty pre-cum. I glide around the vein head, teasing. A deep breath, and I swallow him down. Hot and throbbing in my mouth. Slick with spit. I work my way back and then up again letting his length press the back of my throat until I'm choking. He tests my gag reflex, but that's okay. It'll create more spit. I choke on him until I need to breathe.

I draw back and smile and lick my lips. His hands have whitened where they're holding the bars.

Lowering my head again, I bob on his cock, working into a rhythm. Then I take him deep and hum.

He shouts something in a foreign language. I don't know what, but it sounds like a curse. I grin to myself and take him as deep as I can, pressing my head against the bars. His cock is thick and hard in my mouth. No sign of impending orgasm.

He can't touch me, but he didn't say anything about me touching myself.

Still working his dick, I pull up the top I'm wearing to expose my breasts. I hum as I play with my nipples, rolling them in my fingers until they're needy points. Then I brace one hand on the bars and slip the other into my pants. My fingers touch my wet heat, and I moan.

Gabriel lets out another harsh curse. "No," he orders and fists a hand in my hair. *Alrighty then.* With both hands on the bars, I pull myself on and off his dick. His hips are jerking now, and he uses my hair as a leash to guide me the way he wants. I take him deep and hum some more.

His shaft throbs, and then his hips jerk, rooting him deep in my mouth. He comes, his head thrown back, his dark hair wild, his jaw and entire body clenched. His essence spurts into my mouth, filling it so quickly, I almost choke. I keep humming and drink him down, licking and swallowing as fast as I can.

He pulls out of my mouth and turns away. I touch my puffy lips, missing the feel of him already.

He still has his back to me, his bronzed muscles rippling. He stepped away to get back his control. That's okay. I made him lose it once. I can do it again.

The cage bars lower, spiraling back down into the platform. It's going to take some effort to get to my feet. Stiffness is setting in my body as it remembers how frozen and cold it was.

Gabriel's scent hits me, and he swoops me into his arms. I suppress my smirk at my victory and snuggle into his bare chest.

"Did I do good?" I sound sweet and submissive, but inside I'm cackling. *I won!*

"Yes," his reply is short and clipped, but my spine tingles at the sensation of his lips brushing my hair.

He carries me to an elevator in the corner by the stairs. When the lift begins and he makes no move to set me down, I rest my head on his bare shoulder, feeling dreamy and drowsy.

I blink, and we're back in that high tower bedroom of his, the one from last night. The sun has set, and it's lit by the fire dancing in the stone dragon's mouth and the warm glow of recessed lights.

He lowers me down in the bathroom and turns on the hot water in the bath. He makes quick work of my clothes and sets me into the steaming tub. I hiss as the hot water hits my chilled skin, but melt against the tub side as I quickly warm up. It's a Roman-style bath, big enough for an orgy. I can stretch out my legs. The water is scented, and when I touch the salty bubbles they fizz on my chapped hands.

Gabriel picks up my wrist and frowns at my torn-up palms. He arranges me, so my arms rest on a dry ledge before rising.

"Stay," he orders.

I give him a thumbs up. It's not like I need him to order me to relax. It's a relief to be back in this warm castle after all my climbing excursions. I can soak my sore muscles and think of a new way to escape.

A splash wakes me from a half-asleep state. Gabriel

steps into the bath. He's naked but for a pair of black boxer briefs clinging to his form. Once again, he takes my wrists and slathers some sort of balm all over my hands. His touch is thorough but gentle. It wakes me.

He draws me from the seat ledge deeper into the water and glides behind me. Taking some sort of sea sponge, he starts with my shoulders and rubs the soapy sponge over every inch of me. His large hands move me around like I'm some sort of doll, but he's incredibly gentle. He spends a long time gently dabbing at my hands, cleaning them before coating them with more balm. Then my face and neck, and finally he works his fingers into my hair.

I melt, filled with a sweet ache. He's totally intent, controlled, but attentive. It's hard to resist. If I weren't so blissed out, I'd rip off his boxer briefs and climb onto his lap.

All too soon, he leaves the bath. I soak some more, half asleep, more than halfway to horny. I'm not giving up trying to get away, but part of me wants to know if it'd be so bad to be kept by Gabriel. The sight of his body makes me weak. When he returns, he's in a red and gold silk robe that makes his skin glow. He bundles me in a fluffy towel and carries me to the bed.

Apparently, he's not going to let me walk or move on my own. I'm still drowsy, so I let him position me in his lap. There's a bar cart covered with dishes pulled up to the bed. He lifts the silver dome off a hearty bowl of pasta and meatballs. He shifts me in his lap, so he can reach the spoon. Apparently, he's going to feed me.

"Open," he orders, and I do. He feeds me with the same concentrated attention as he bathed me. And I let him.

With food, my energy comes back. I push up off Gabriel's chest. His arms tighten around me, but he lets me angle myself in his lap, partly facing him. "This is nice," I say as my belly fills. I finger the richly patterned sleeve of his robe. Red and gold, the shimmering color of his dragon scales. "Do you like these colors because you're the same color when you're a dragon?"

"Perhaps." Gabriel looks so serious. His hair is combed back again, sleek and somehow dry even though he just took a bath with me. He's all put together again. Stern and back in control. I want to make a mess of him.

"You can turn invisible, I remember. That's how you grabbed me in the desert."

"When I revealed myself to you, you fainted."

"I assumed as much. Why didn't you tell me when I first woke?"

"I thought it best to ease you into this slowly."

I'm loose and languid on his lap, but his body is rigid, his dark brows knotted together. I reach up and rub away the wrinkle at the bridge of his nose, trying to relax him.

His sigh blows back the freshly dried tendrils of my hair. "I thought then you would want to be with me and not want to escape."

"Take notes, Dr. Jekyll. When a guy kidnaps me, I'm always going to want to escape. I am not the sort of woman who can be kept."

My mother is. She freaking lived for that sort of arrangement.

And that's why I'm allergic to it.

"Even when I give you everything you need?"

I shrug. "Even then." Although it is nice to be pampered. Gabriel seems to want to meet my needs.

He reaches up and fists a hand in my hair, tugging hard before massaging the sting away. "You should not have run. You could've been hurt."

"The escape route was right there. I couldn't not try after your dragon showed me everything."

"Dragon?" Gabriel snarls. He turns my head, so I'm pinned by his amber gaze. "He showed you how to escape?"

Caught in his grip, I give an insolent shrug. "Yes, in my dream. Every detail."

Gabriel loosens his fingers. "Not only did he speak to you, but he tried to help you escape me." A desolate note enters his voice. "He hasn't spoken to me in many years."

I reach down, find his wrist and circle it with my fingers the way the gold cuff circles mine. "Maybe because you cuff him. Keep him captive."

Gabriel's gaze is unfocused. I dip my head close to catch his attention. "If you love someone, set them free, Gabriel." I am this close to busting into the Sting song's chorus.

His expression hardens. "It's too dangerous."

"Well, get used to escape attempts, buddy."

"No. You will not make such a foolish attempt again." He lifts me off the bed. I tussle with him halfheartedly, and he easily overpowers me. My body is warmed by the bath and heat of his body, and energy crackles between us, that explosive combination of our beings. The alchemy we have that leads to sex or fighting or both.

A machine whirrs, and he sets me down against something solid. A St. Andrew's cross. I only know because…well, I read kinky books. My wrists and ankles magnetize to the metal.

He steps close to tie my hair back.

"These are trackers," I nod to my wrists.

"Yes." He sounds as smug as I felt before. "If you think you will escape me, you are mistaken. If you run, I'll chase you to the ends of the earth."

"We'll see about that." I lean back, offering up my body even though I'm tethered to on the cross. He thinks he's won, but I still have some tricks up my sleeve. "Do your worst."

He goes to the bar cart and pours himself a drink. "You're not afraid of me." It's not a question.

"Nope." I toss my head.

He studies me, sipping at a glass filled with amber liquid.

After a stint in a nudist commune and a modeling career, I'm immune to being naked. What bothers me is that he hasn't been fully naked around me. Yet.

He hasn't kissed me. Hasn't had sex with me. He holds himself back. Controls all of our interactions. It's getting old.

But being bound on the cross is doing things to me. My pussy was already stimulated by his gentle washing in the bath, and now it swells with need. My nipples are hard and pointy in the open air.

He puts the glass to my lips. Smooth alcohol burns down my throat. I get a tiny taste of the cognac before he pulls the glass away. "Then it's time for your punishment." He sets the glass down with a decisive click.

I'm not afraid, but my tummy flutters with anticipation.

"You need to know: You cannot escape me. The sooner you learn this, the easier it will be."

"Like I said before. If you try to control me, I will always run from you. You might have tracking devices on me, but I will figure out a way around that too. Maybe I'll just ask the dragon. We can free each other."

His eyes change, the irises lengthening to vertical slits. "He won't let you go, either. The dragon is dangerous. You should not speak to him."

"You can't control what we can or can't do," I tell him. My tone might be a little smug.

A thin stream of mist trails from his nostrils. He doesn't like that.

"So what are you going to do now that you've got me tied up?" I taunt. "Whip me? Flog me?" I try to hide my shiver.

Gabriel sees my excitement. He sees everything. "No. You'd enjoy that too much. There are better ways to ensure your compliance."

"Really? I—" But I can't speak anymore because he's crossed to me in a blur of movement, and his fingers fill my mouth, pressing on my tongue, stopping all speech.

"Suck," he commands. I do. I curl my tongue around and deep throat his fingers until my head rocks back.

He tugs my right nipple with his free hand and cups my pussy with his wet hand. Three fingers, thrust into my aching channel. I'd rise to tiptoes but the cross holds me still. He's rubbing me, and there's some sort of extraordinary heat in his fingers. "You will give yourself to me."

Pleasure coils tight deep in my belly. I'm panting.

"It would be so easy to submit. It will feel so good."

His fingers hit the right spot, and I whimper.

His eyes go dark. "You will submit to me."

"Never," I breathe, but it's not going to be never. If he keeps rubbing me this way, it's going to be like five minutes.

His fingers dip into my pussy, collecting liquid and sweeping it up to rub it over my back door. I try to shift out of the way, but there's no escaping his touch. It feels good, and I'm just going to have to take it.

"Does it feel good?"

I duck my head, but he grips my hair with his free hand, forcing me to face him.

"Why do you even want me to submit to you?" I gasp.

"I've waited centuries for you," he growls, and the whole castle seems to shake. "There is no one else for me. If you run, I will rip apart this world to find you. There is no place you can hide from me."

"Oh God." I'm so close to coming. A few more seconds, a slightly harder pressure...

"You will submit to me."

My head shakes back and forth.

"Give yourself to me, Tabitha. It will be so easy."

He takes his hands away. My orgasm ebbs to nothing.

"You bastard," I whisper.

He turns away, chuckling. I strain, but I can't break free from the binds.

Gabriel returns and smooths my hair out of my face.

"Give me your cock." I lick my lips.

His eyes hood. "No."

"I'm not going to beg," I warn.

There's a buzzing sound, and he presses a toy to my clit at just the right spot.

"Pleasepleasepleasepleaseplease!"

He chuckles again, the bastard. The sensation is too much. My orgasm's going to hit me like a bomb. I writhe, trying to get away.

But when I'm right on the edge, he draws the vibrator away.

"Fuck me!" My orgasm ebbs away and dies.

"No." His lips curve under his beard, beautiful and cruel.

"I hate you."

"No, you don't." He replaces the toy with his fingers, gentle and teasing. It's somehow worse than the toy. His skin emanates warmth, like the blast of heat upon opening an oven.

He takes me to the edge, again and again, using his fingers and the toy to manipulate me to the brink of orgasm, but he never lets me go over. A drop of sweat rolls down the valley of my breasts. My heaving chest has a silky sheen.

Every now and again, he stops and gives me careful sips of water. He's most devastating like this, up close, holding a glass to my lips and pressing a cool cloth to my heated skin. He attaches some sort of harness that holds a vibrator against my pussy, and leaves me to sip his own drink. In his robe, with not a hair out of place, he's the picture of poise and arrogance. He never takes his eyes off me.

The vibrator buzzes on low. I try to angle my hips, so it hits the right spot, but there's not enough sensation for me to come.

"You will break."

"Promises, promises."

He returns to fondle my nipples, Pinching and pulling, rolling each one between his fingers. He leans close, his lips finding my ear. My legs tremble to close, so I can come with his heat and scent rolling over me.

"Submit to me."

I shake my head.

He steps away and stalks around the cross. A new toy buzzes. He presses it to my backdoor. I clench my ass against the vibrations, but it's futile. The sensation only increases the need in my pussy.

I writhe and sweat when he takes both the toys and harness away.

"Gabriel," I moan. I'm half out of my mind.

"I'm right here, my treasure." He's back in front, facing me, brushing back my hair. He strokes it back and massages my neck, stroking me like a cat.

"I need to see you. All of you." He's always in clothes, even when I'm naked before him.

His hand cups the back of my neck. "What will you give me for a glimpse?"

"It'll make me happy."

"I want to make you happy. Just say the word. Say you belong to me."

Smoke caresses my face. I blink at the gold light in his eyes. His pupils have changed.

I grin. "Hello, dragon."

He growls, and the castle shudders. The earth quakes with a seismic shift, as if it recognizes him as master.

"You think I'm yours?" I strain forward to brush his lips. He doesn't allow the kiss. "Then prove it. Fuck me."

"Tell me you're mine."

"Fine. I'm yours." *For now.*

7

Gabriel

I push a button and turn off the vibrator and release the magnets on her wrists. Tabitha's arms fall downwards, and she slumps as the magnets holding her release.

I catch my mate and carry her to the bed, turning her face down with her feet almost touching the floor.

When she tries to reposition herself, I smack her ass. I need the control here. Fucking her from behind should help me. Keep me from claiming her.

I prop up her hips and free my erection to slide into her. She's juicy wet, her flesh swollen and ready. The bed is the right height for me to drive into her. It feels good.

Perfect.

Delicious.

I fist a hand in her hair, and she bows backward, arching into a half-circle.

She plants her hands and pushes back as if to take every centimeter of my dick.

I growl, and she shivers and snarls back. Her enthusiasm pushes the limits of my control. If I'm not careful, she will completely wreck me.

With every thrust, she clenches on my cock. My hands grip her hips to hold her still for my battering ram of cock. She tips forward, rubbing her needy clit against the bed.

Fate, I can't take it. She's too much. Too perfect. She's undoing me.

I pull out and crack my palm against her upturned ass, punishing her for being such a damn temptation. Such a torment to me. She flips her hair and looks over her shoulder at me, her teeth bared like she's the wild beast, not me.

I spank her again and again, loving the way the sound fills the room. Her little cries followed by labored breath.

She snarls and flips around. My beautiful unabashed female. She wants it all from me, but I can't give it.

I have to stay in control. I won't claim her with my fire until I'm certain I can do it without causing her harm.

Desperate to maintain control—of myself, of my bride, of everything—I wrestle her down, pinning her by her delicate wrists to the bed.

"Take off your clothes," she demands, her eyes lit with the glow of the fire, as if she's a dragoness and not a delicate, docile human. "Why are you still wearing that goddamn fancy robe?"

I am still in the robe, but the tie's undone, and it gapes open in the front. She drinks in the sight of my bare chest like she's starved for it.

"At least your hair is mussed for once."

I don't have the brain capacity to decode her meaning—why she wants my hair mussed and dislikes my robe so much. Too much of my blood has traveled south to my other head.

Tabitha still fights me for control, wrapping her legs

around my waist and pulling me into her. I forget to hold her down, and she gets a hand free and grips my cock.

I nearly come from her touch alone. A shudder runs through me, the fire in my Mercurial center flaring hot and sending steam billowing from my nostrils.

Tabitha guides me in. "Fuck me," she orders and digs her nails through the robe into the heavy heaving muscles of my back.

I'm losing my mind. The flames of need and desire take over.

"You're so hot," Tabitha moans as I thrust into her.

I force myself to slow the thrusts. To pull back and look at her face. "Too hot? Do I burn you, my love?"

She rolls her head on the bedcovers, her eyes glassy and bright. "No, no, no, no, no. Not too hot. Stop stopping. I mean, don't stop, dragon." She grips the lapels of my robe and yanks me down, her sweet lips seeking mine for a kiss.

I bury my head against her neck, instead, letting my teeth graze her skin.

"I need you," she sobs.

My dragon goes wild within me, the desire to satisfy our mate too strong.

I stop moving, closing my eyes to force him back into his chains. Into the golden cuffs that keep him locked safely away.

"Stop stopping!" she screams, beating her fists on my shoulders, even as her legs yank my hips closer.

She thinks I'm teasing her still, denying her orgasm.

I pretend it's so. I lift my head and give her a smug look.

She certainly deserves the torture after what she put me through. Risking her life like that.

She deserves to be punished all week.

Her frenzied gaze seeks mine. "Please."

I'm incapable of denying her. I resume thrusting, making her body rock with each instroke.

"Your muscles are like stones heated on a fire." She grips me, fighting to be closer. She rocks her hips up to meet each thrust, taking me deeper. "I need to feel it. I need to feel it all."

"Gabriel. I need you. No more Mr. Control." She cranes her neck and nips at my shoulder.

I shudder and buck, fucking her hard enough to send her through the bed.

"Come on, come on," she chants, locking her ankles over my back. She arches her back and writhes against me, rubbing her nipples over my robe and chest.

I find her G-spot with my cock, and she snaps. She shakes and trembles, her cry turning to a keening pitch as she bounces with every savage snap of my hips.

My dragon's growl reverberates in the room, and the castle shudders at the power of it.

Fuck.

My skin glows from the fire stemming from my power center, but brightest around his heart. "Come, Tabitha," I order in a guttural voice. I shove in deep and stay, using every ounce of will I have not to come myself. Not to let loose the seed that will brand her womb. The essence that will brand her soul. The fire that will forever mark her as mine.

Tabitha cries out, her muscles squeezing and contracting around my cock. "Are you coming?" she gasps, as if I'm not struggling enough to hold back.

I hold still, keeping my body tense and tight, crushing down the urgent need to tear and thrash and roar with fire over not claiming my tantalizing mate.

The moment Tabitha's orgasm completes I pull out and pump my fist over my cock, spilling my cum on her belly and thighs.

She pants like she's trying to catch her breath. She appears dazed and delirious from the love-making.

When she's caught her breath, her brow knits. "Why won't you come inside me? Is it part of the control-issue thing?"

I smear my essence up between her breasts, needing at least some form of branding her as mine. I'm relieved to find it's not too hot. I smooth my expression. "Perhaps."

"Even that answer is controlling! What is your deal?" She pushes up on her elbows and sends me an accusing look. Of all the things I just did to her–trapping her in a cage, edging her, turning her ass a pretty shade of pink–the thing she's upset about is me not coming inside her?

I...don't understand this female.

She falls back on the pillows. "You can't keep me, Gabriel," she says stubbornly. "You can't control everything. You can't control *me*."

I climb onto the bed and turn her to face away from me, so I can spoon her. She's exhausted, and I need to hold her until she falls asleep. She lets me. Even though her words and tone hold frustration, she doesn't push me away. Doesn't fight me.

No, the problem is more nuanced than I imagined.

She seems to want something I'm incapable of giving her.

My passion.

My completion.

My dragon. All of me.

I caress her soft skin with my palm, cupping her breast and brushing my lips across her temple. I won't spend the night with her—I know I can't—but I need to try to somehow soothe her irritation.

"I'm sorry, my treasure. But I can't let you go."

8

Amber

Winters in Tucson aren't cold, but they're still chilly. Usually, my mate Garrett is the one riding around on his bike in nothing but jeans, a t-shirt, and a leather vest, while I bundle up like I'm about to go skiing. But today, I'm outside on the patio in nothing but yoga pants and a light sweater.

A soft whisper is my only warning that the screen door is opening behind me. For such a huge guy, my boyfriend moves as quietly as a cat. Not that I'd ever vocally compare him to a cat. Not unless we were in a fight, and I was really, really mad.

"Hey babe," Garrett's voice rumbles a second before he nuzzles my neck. "Aren't you cold?"

My lips curve, and I reach back to pull him close. He seats himself beside me, propping his boots on the concrete table and plucking my book off my lap with his big tattooed hands.

When I first saw Garrett, he scared the hell out of me. He was huge, covered in tats, a rugged motorcycle man riding on the edge of what could be considered criminal. The last sort of person I would hang out with.

Now my fingers itch to trace his tattoos.

"Nope, not cold. Not anymore."

Garrett pulls my legs into his lap and closes a hand over one of my socked feet. "When I met you, you were always cold in the winter."

"I remember." I would buy him sweaters just to steal them in the winter.

He raises a brow and reads my mind. "You're always stealing my sweatshirts."

"You love it when I steal your sweatshirts," I return. Especially when I wear them and nothing else. It's such a change from my typical uptight lawyer self, it turns him on his head.

"There's a reason I'm not cold this winter." I lean back and let Garrett rub my feet as I rest my hand on my swelling belly. "This one turned me into an oven."

"Is that what babies do?"

"That's what he does."

"You mean she?" he shoots back.

I shake my head. "I think he's a boy. Mothers always know." It's really a girl—I've had visions of her from the beginning and had an ultrasound yesterday to confirm. I'm going to tell him tonight—but I love it when we argue. It's the lawyer in me.

Garrett isn't fooled. "You know I can tell when you lie?"

I just grin at him. He rolls his eyes but keeps massaging my foot with delicious pressure.

"Why are you home so early? Not that I'm complaining."

His expression turns sober. "I got a request from the Taos pack."

I sit up as straight as I can with my feet in his lap. "Taos? Who do we know in Taos?"

"Alpha named Rafe Lightfoot. He just found his mate. Another human." His eyes crinkle.

"Humans do make the best mates," I tease. "You can't resist us."

"That's right." He squeezes my foot. "But it seems like one of his mate's good friends is missing. A woman named Tabitha. She's a wanderer, but she said she'd probably check in for Christmas, and she hasn't. She also hasn't made it to her destination."

"Okay." I snap into serious mode.

"The guys are checking with Kylie to hack her phone to see if they can find her that way. But they asked a favor of you." He hesitates.

"They want me to try to get a reading on her."

"Yeah." My mate looks reluctant to continue, and I know why.

"It's okay." I don't typically volunteer to use my psychic gifts, but I don't try to suppress them like I used to. With Garrett's help, I've realized my visions are a gift, not a curse. So I might as well use them. "I want to help."

"I figured you would. They're mailing a box of her stuff. But Rafe sent over something he had on hand. Tabitha made this by hand." He pulls out a plastic sleeve and hands it to me.

Inside is a cream-colored scarf.

I swing my legs down and scoot around, so I'm no longer touching Garrett. His arms are out by his side like he wants to touch me, but he holds off.

I inhale and tip the sleeve and let the scarf flutter into my hand.

Redfireheatlongingexplosionflame!

I cry out.

"Amber! Baby, talk to me." Garrett kneels next to me. His big hands wrap around mine. Each of his fingers are tattooed with a different stage of the waxing and waning moon. I often trace them when I'm upset. They ground me.

I touch the crescent moon. "I'm okay."

He fumbles with my bottle of water as he hands it to me. I'm trying to stay hydrated.

"Are you sure you're okay?"

I nod. The baby kicks me hard in the spleen. "Oof." I press on my stomach until the natal Can-Can subsides.

Garret's eyes are wild. "Is the baby okay?"

"She's fine," I say quickly.

He shakes his head. "Knew it was a girl."

I try to smile but can only blow out a shaky breath.

He wraps a big hand around the back of my neck and tips his forehead to touch mine. For a second, we stay like that, breathing together.

"I'm good." I lift my head. "It just caught me by surprise." I cough a little as Garrett rubs my back. It feels like I've inhaled soot. It's scratching the back of my throat.

"Baby." The scarf has fallen to my feet. He picks it up and tosses it away. "You don't have to go through that again."

"It's okay. I want to help. It was just that the vision came on so strong."

What did you see? He doesn't ask, but the question is reflected in his eyes.

I take a shaky breath. "I saw fire. Nothing but fire."

∼

Tabitha

I fall into the dream like it's been waiting for me. I'm back in the warm darkness, the pleasing smell of smoky incense surrounding me. A lamp glows over my head. Piles of ancient coins shimmer in the distance like a desert mirage. A shadow moves and becomes the dragon. The huge neck curves around, and his head appears high above me.

Hello there, *I say.*

The huge wedge head descends. The dragon chuffs his own hello. The hot breath blows back the robe I'm wearing, making the fabric swirl around my ankles. I smooth down folds. The brocade is red and gold. You like these colors don't you? And you like seeing me in them.

The robe bears the pattern—rows and rows of Borromean rings. Each of the dragon's scales bears their own set of interlocking circles. Three rings that can never be broken.

Is this your sigil? *I stretch a fold between my hands to show the dragon.* Your crest?

A fallen scale glimmers at my feet. I pick up the scale and hug it to my chest.

What are we going to do about Gabriel? *I ask sadly.*

The dragon doesn't answer.

He says I shouldn't talk to you. He's mad about the escape, but you just wanted to help me, right? *I lean against the dragon's arm, tracing the symbol on the scale I hold. I want to help you.* It's not fair that he took both our freedom.

Even in the dream, I feel the constricting grip of Gabriel's control. He won't let me get close to him. He won't let me in. Not like you.

I let the scale fall. I wish I could carry it from my dream, keep a piece of the dragon with me. I'm closer to you than I am to him, *I admit to the dragon.*

The dragon huffs. A warm puff of air stirs my hair.

What happens if I decide Gabriel can't claim me? If I say no?

The dragon rears back its head. There's a rush of heat. Death. Doom. The cave around us rumbles. I thrash, trying to break free of the dream, but my limbs turn to concrete. I cannot escape the vision—the blinding red of a dragon's rage, the breath-stealing heat. The cave disappears, and so does the castle, the village, the world. Screams echo and die, leaving no sound but crackling flame. The world disappears. There's nothing but heat and ash and pain.

Nothing but fire.

～

ONCE AGAIN I wake up alone in my own bedroom. Goddamn Gabriel, giving me an epic night and leaving me in the morning. I'm still naked but my body is refreshed. The bath did its good. My hands look a lot better because of that balm.

There's a lingering tightness in my chest. I try, but can't remember my dreams. Too bad. I could use another powwow with the dragon.

Judging by the light streaming in from the windows, I slept a lot. Yesterday was something else. My escape, meeting the dragon, the cage. Gabriel's delicious way of punishing me.

My stomach gurgles. Dinner filled me up, but I could eat a full English after last night's exertion. When I swing my legs over the side of the bed, there's a twinge in my core. I'm a little sore in the best way.

Unlike yesterday, there's no outfit laid out for me. There is a note in exquisite handwriting that looks like it was inked with a quill pen.

Good morning, my treasure. I hope you slept well. You will rest today and remain in your room. Meals will be delivered to you. Tonight I will come to you. Signed simply *Gabriel.*

Typically Gabriel bossiness. I would toss the note in the fire, but the penmanship is a work of art.

I head to the bathroom to do my business and examine myself carefully in a floor-to-ceiling gilt-framed mirror. My pussy is a little puffy but there is a disappointing lack of hickies. *Too bad.* It'd be nice to see a few red marks from a tight grip or sexy spanking. I've always craved rough sex, and Gabriel is just the one I'd want to get wild with. What would it take for him to lose control?

My second stop is the closet for clothes. The lights flicker on, but instead of the gorgeous fashion display, there are empty cubbies, empty racks, and empty shelves.

What the fuck? I rap my fist on an empty shelf and double-check the built-in closets. There's nothing. Not even a stray hanger.

Out in the bedroom, a bright ringing sound blares. I dash out, grabbing a sheet to wrap around me in case a bunch of servants are about to burst in with my breakfast. But the ringing sound comes from an old-fashioned rotary phone sitting on my bedside table.

I pick it up. "Hello?"

"Good morning, my treasure," Gabriel purrs. "How did you sleep?"

"Great, I snarl. "Where the hell are my clothes?"

"I had them removed."

"What?" I screech. "Bring them back."

He chuckles. My toes curl at the dark and throaty sound.

"I'm serious, Gabriel. What am I supposed to wear?"

"You will earn the right to wear clothing when you obey me."

"Excuse me?" My voice is low and calm. Gabriel will learn that when I get mad, I get quiet because I'm internally plotting on how to destroy him.

"You will remain naked by my whim or as long as you wish. I will have you submit to me, my bride."

I stuff down a growl. "This is not the way to make me happy, Gabriel."

"You were content enough last night," he says smugly.

I strangle my whimper. My pussy throbs between my legs. Apparently, nothing fazes my libido. The angrier I get, the more my attraction to Gabriel grows.

"You can earn your clothing with good behavior."

"You will regret this."

"I'm looking forward to it. I love to play games." Before I think of a reply he continues in a brisk tone, "Your breakfast will be delivered shortly. I have duties today, but you will dine with me this evening."

"That's what you think," I mutter. Not exactly an epic rejoinder, but it's the best I can do. I'm already thinking of what dinner will be like, with me naked and him clothed. Maybe I should give myself some orgasms before then, to take the edge off.

No!

"Oh Tabitha," he says in a perfectly pleasant, even tone. "We will be dining together. Whether you sit with me at my table. Or whether I tie you down to the bed and eat your sweet pussy until you scream. One way or another, you will be dining with me. Tonight."

Before I can pick myself up from where I've melted on the floor, he hangs up.

"Whatever, dragon daddy," I tell the ringtone and slam the ringer down.

I gather up the sheet I draped around me. Gabriel thinks he's got the upper hand, but this is just another obstacle to scale.

I eye the bed curtains. I've spent the last few years using my seamstress skills to upcycle clothes for a living. I could do a *Sound of Music* "How do you solve a problem like Maria" montage, but it would be a shame to slice up these beautiful drapes.

I drape the bed sheet around me like a toga, using hair ties and some pins Gabriel forgot to remove from the bathroom drawers.

Breakfast has still not arrived when I head back into the bedroom. The door is locked, but a few tries with a straightened hairpin takes care of it. My mother tried to control me with locked doors, too.

I creep into the hall. The air is cool on my mostly bare skin.

Any minute now someone might come up with breakfast, so I left the bathroom door shut with the lights on and fans blowing inside. Maybe it'll fool them for a little bit. But probably not for long with these trackers on my wrists. Gabriel probably can look me up and see where I'm going. So I better hurry.

I don't have a plan of escape. The key, I think, will be getting Gabriel to make a mistake. So far Mr. Control Freak hasn't let down his guard with me. The closest he came was letting me give him a blowjob while I was in the cage. And even that he controlled as much as possible.

Time to turn his life upside down. First item of business: get some clothes. Second item of business: create mayhem. And, if possible, escape.

I follow the winding hall until I find the suit of armor that was my landmark before. The window is sealed shut, and a grate of iron bars cover the outside. Gabriel works fast. He must have an army of servants to keep this castle running. Or robots. Or both.

Out of the corner of my eye, a lick of fire seems to dance on a doorknob. When I turn, it's disappeared, but I know better than to ignore my instinct's nudges. I slip over and pick the lock.

The door swings open before me, and a light blinks on. The scent of mothballs reaches me. I'm in a parlor sort of room bookended with two floor-to-ceiling gilt-framed mirrors. The space is filled with racks and racks of clothes.

I grab the closest thing to me, a red and gold robe a lot like the one Gabriel was wearing last night. It makes sense that he has a few of these to lounge in when he's not wearing his Brioni suits. The robe reaches my ankles, and I have to roll up the sleeves, but when I tie the sash as tight as I can around me, I look pretty good.

Time for the next phase of the plan. Create mayhem? Or more exploring to find some food? I'm not going back to my bedroom. My stomach rumbles, giving its opinion.

I need to keep moving.

When I step out of the bedroom, there's an amber glow at the end of the hall. Not coming from a lamp or any light source. This is another sign. I don't hesitate, I head towards the light, following it down a long hall to where it forks, and choose which way to go by following the light again. One thing I've learned from being cooped up in this castle: don't ignore my psychic gifts. I've never been so quick to follow my visions or intuition before.

The glow leads me down a stone staircase and up another. I'm in a different part of the castle. The air is colder. The carpet, older and faded. After one turn, the modern molding and drywall disappear, leaving only the stone pavers and exposed wooden beams of the original castle. Medieval shabby chic. The hall twists and turns, intersecting with others like a maze.

My vision better lead me back the way I came; otherwise, I'm going to be lost.

I round a corner and the glow has disappeared.

Well, fuck.

I'm in a long, drafty hall. The only buffer from the chilly stone walls is a huge red and gold tapestry, unfolding in stages. There have been plenty of tapestries at the auctions I've attended, but this one is the oldest and most well preserved specimen I've seen. Each panel tells a story. To the left, where the colors are most faded, is a forest scene with all sorts of animals. A lion, a lamb, a faun, a unicorn, all clustered around a huge golden egg.

The story continues left to right. In the next panel, yellow shards of the egg lie around a tiny red lizard-like figure. The fauns and unicorns and rest of the creatures are cavorting around the baby dragon. There are a few panels documenting the red dragon's growth, culminating with him on top of a mountain, blowing a plume of fire into a blue sky. His red scales have a touch of gold thread. More gold thread lines the bottom of the tapestry panel, depicting piles of gold.

Hello, Gabriel.

The central panel is a portrait of Gabriel. Dark hair, short beard, long red and gold robe like the one I'm wearing. Gold thread for his eyes. In his left hand is a book, and in his right, he holds golden scales. A wise and learned rich guy.

Then we're back in the forest. There's a bunch of peasants cavorting about, some dancing, some with musical instruments, some carrying a bridal bower. And in the center is a Madonna-type woman with long hair and a halo around her head. Instead of the usual gold or cream-colored glow, the light bubble is rich purple. *Kinda like my aura.* She has long brown hair like me too. She also wears golden cuffs around her wrists, marked with a stylized image of a dragon.

My hand rises of its own volition, wanting to touch her.

And then the images on the rest of the tapestry begin to move. My vision, bringing them to life. The happy scene fades into a scene of destruction. The forest is burning. The animals are running away or dead on the ground. And the wedding party is freaking out. The central figure, the woman, is gone. In her place is a plume of gold fire, blown from a huge red-eyed dragon.

The dragon grows bigger and bigger, blocking everything else out. And then: Nothing but fire, so hot that my face burns like I've stuck it in an oven.

The fire fades, revealing a barren wasteland. In the center stands a dark-haired man, all alone, in a ring of fire. There's a pair of golden cuffs on the ground.

A cold wind blows up my back.

"Madam?"

I turn, almost relieved to hear the crisp accent of Buttons. "Good morning."

Buttons bows. He's holding a silver tray with a covered dish. "Good morning to you. May I serve you breakfast?"

I give my hair a toss. "I'll be dining in the kitchen again this morning," I tell him loftily, daring him to disagree. Somehow I can't imagine Buttons chasing me down this hall or wrestling me back into my room if I put up a fight.

After a moment of hesitation, he bows his head. "Of course, madame."

~

Gabriel

"Wolf Security has put out a search for Ms. Tabitha, sir," Andrei Hess, my head of security reports.

"As expected."

I knew the wolves would look eventually. I've seen the calls and texts come through on Tabitha's phone from her friends. At first, they were friendly queries, but it seemed they expected to hear from her over Christmas and did not.

Of course, I had location tracking removed from her phone and have disabled it completely, so I receive her notifications on an untraceable computer network only. They won't find her through the phone.

They probably will find her through me. Or they will try, anyway.

The wolves have attempted to break into one of my fortresses before. Of course, I was waiting for them. I knew they were coming and what would be important to them. I sent them scrambling to protect their mates to keep them off my trail.

I will be ready for them when they come for Tabitha, too.

I don't feel my usual glee at the cat and mouse game, though. Because Tabitha is the prize at stake this time. And she's far too precious to me to take any risks. If my dragon believes she's threatened, I could lose control. Rampage and burn down the entire castle with my sweet treasure in it.

For that reason, I cannot allow them to find her. If I have to move her all over the world to stay ahead of them, I'll do it.

Of course, the better solution would be for Tabitha to accept me as her mate. For me to win her trust and she mine, so I can give her a phone back, and she can put her friends' minds at ease.

But alas, we are not there yet.

I'm not sure if my locking her naked in her room today helps or hinders.

I do know the thought of it has my cock rock hard in anticipation of seeing her again.

Sex is the one area Tabitha will play with me, so I intend to continue this game as she enjoys it.

I realize Hess is still standing there, waiting for orders. "Let me know the moment any of them leave their compound."

"I am monitoring all their movements," Hess agrees.

"Be prepared to neutralize any threats, but only with non-lethal means."

Hess hesitates. "Wouldn't it be better to simply…eliminate the threat? I could strike their compound in Taos and–"

"*No.* I don't want any of them killed. They are friends of my bride. She would not forgive such an outcome. But I cannot have them interfering in our courtship."

"Understood. The lab is working on the high-potency tranquilizer that should work to keep a shifter down long enough to put him in silver chains."

"Good."

I hesitate.

"Hess."

"Yes, sir?"

"I want you to make a dose strong enough for a dragon, as well."

He goes still, his Siberian tiger eyes glowing yellow with awareness. "For you, sir?"

I blow out a breath. "If my dragon believes my mate is at risk, he could rampage. I can't risk…"

"I see," Hess cuts in at once.

"You're the only one who should have access to that dosage, and I only authorize you to use it if my mate is in danger. Understand?"

"Perfectly."

"I don't even want anyone else to know of its existence."

"I will need an approximate weight."

A weight. Fuck. I need to find a semi-truck scale somewhere. "I will get it for you."

"And points of vulnerability."

Everything in my body rebels. A dragon does not reveal his weaknesses. Not to anyone.

How sure of Hess am I?

And yet, this is Tabitha's safety we're talking about.

It's of utmost importance.

I lift my chin and point to the soft spot between throat and jaw. "Here." I sense the dragon rebelling within me. A restless, angry stirring. A stream of steam flows from my nostrils. I lift my arm and point to the soft space there. "And here."

I pin him with a look. "You tell another soul, and I'll rip your limbs off and send them to your mother."

"I owe you my life," he says, a note of fierceness in his voice. I freed him from a shifter slaving operation I took down eight years ago. He hasn't left my side since although I have paid him well enough to start a new life.

"Your loyalty will always be rewarded."

He gives me a bow because his kung fu training ingrained that form of respect into him despite his years of torture in a cage.

When he leaves, I pull up the tracker app. Technology is so useful. Of all the dragons I know, I've been the most eager to embrace the power modernity affords me. But I've always been obsessed with power.

And now, I'm obsessed with Tabitha. My bride. The damn trackers did me no good yesterday when she was escaping because I'd been too agitated to remain in my human form.

Thank fate, my dragon somehow sensed she needed help.

They have some kind of connection.

How ironic.

The very part of me I'm trying to keep from her, to protect her from, is the only part she seems to like.

Well, perhaps not the only part. I smile remembering how she begged me last night.

Even though I know she's safely locked in her chamber, I check her location on my tracker app.

Malediction!

The blinking light that signals her presence is on the other side of the castle. Down in the kitchen levels.

My claws elongate. My eyes are probably slitted like a snake's. I thunder through the castle, slamming doors, making my presence known.

Soft smoky laughter drifts up the stairs from the servant's quarters. I slow on the steps.

Tabitha is in the kitchen, sitting on a stool at the low, worn wood table. My chef and butler are feeding and entertaining her. She laughs again, and the musical sound soothes me to the depth of my soul.

She's wearing my robe. She escaped from her room and found it somehow. *Clever mate.*

Her skin glows in the firelight and the red and gold of the robe. She was born to wear my colors.

Satisfaction curls through me, making me pause in the door. I could bask in her light forever.

But this behavior requires correction.

~

Tabitha

I sense Gabriel before I see him.

I don't know how long I've been here, sitting on the stool and listening to Giampi's stories about his *nonna*. The short, curly-haired Italian chef is hilarious. Even Buttons–who I now know as James–has a dry wit that cracks me up.

My stomach is full, I'm warm and settled, but there's a little flutter in my chest. Like a compass needle, always searching for its true north.

I swivel on my chair, and there he is, standing in the doorway, looking like he wants to punish me all over again. Or eat me out and feed me his cum.

Probably all three.

Chef Giampi and James greet him, but he has eyes for only me.

"Hello, dragon," I say.

"Leave us," he orders softly, and Chef Giampi and James exit the room right away.

Smoke streams from his nostrils. His hands glitter as if his skin is about to turn to scales. He moves forward, and a wave of heat hits my skin.

I duck my head close and inhale the rich incense of his scent. "You smell like him. The dragon."

"Did you dream of him last night?"

"Oh yes. We hung out. At this point, I like him better than you."

"That's definitely a first. Most people are terrified of him."

"I'm not most people."

"I'm beginning to understand this." He's still staring at me. My body's about to internally combust.

I half turn and stick my finger in a dish. Turns out it's pate. It would be sexier if it was whipped cream, but oh well. I lick the earthy-tasting cream off my fingers as sexily as I can.

His eyes follow my every movement. "You disobeyed me. I told you to stay in your room."

I shrug. "I wanted to get out of my room. So I got myself out."

"I see." His voice is dangerously low. He's like me, he gets quiet when he's mad. "And you came to the kitchens?"

"Yes." I'm not going to throw Buttons under the bus. Let Gabriel think I figured out my way down here on my own. "It was nice to have a conversation with decent people."

He prowls closer. "What did you talk about?"

"You, actually."

He stops a foot away, his brow knotting. "Did you find out anything interesting?"

I shrug. "They didn't tell me anything embarrassing. They think you're a god."

He raises a black brow.

"Not a god. But a really great boss. They raved about you. You showed up, refurbished the castle. Gave jobs to all the villagers in a thirty-mile radius. Revived an artisan pottery factory. Paid for new roads, fixed bridges. And apparently, you hold a fancy ball to celebrate Christmas. The Orthodox date in January. This year, it'll be held on the ninth."

"That's true."

"You're a regular benevolent lord of the castle. A modern-day 'Good King Wenceslas.'"

He snorts. "Duke Vaclav wouldn't lift a finger for another."

"Oooh, he was a poser? Of course, you would know. You're an anachronism."

I lean against the island to look up at him. He leans in, setting his arms on either side of me.

"We need to address your continued disobedience."

"What are you going to do about it?" I ask. "Old man," I add.

He leans back. I suck in a breath. We're caught in the split second when I've stepped over the side of the cliff and realized I'm about to fall.

He whirls me around and clamps a hand to the back of my neck, pinning my front to the butcher block. He yanks off the sash of the robe. My arms are caught in the sleeves, and the robe bunches up in the back, baring my butt.

He palms my left buttock. "I think you wanted to disobey me. I think you want me to truly punish you." His hand claps down on my ass. "I think you like it."

"Maybe, I do," I pant.

"Take this like a good girl," he purrs. "And I will give you a reward."

I press myself into the butcher block, presenting my bottom to him.

This time he spanks me with something other than his hand. I yelp. The smaller surface area stings. I look back. There's a bright red mark on my backside, and Gabriel's wielding a wooden spoon.

What Chef Giampi doesn't know won't hurt him.

He smacks me with the spoon, marking my right buttock with a similar mark. Though it hurts, I bend back over. I want these marks. My body has been electrified since the moment I woke in this castle. I'm needy, craving sex and stimulation. Always desperate for satisfaction.

He braces me with a hand on my hip, kicks my feet further apart, and taps the implement against my pussy.

Even though it was a light tap, it's intense, and my shout rings out, bouncing off the stove and tiled walls.

I try to close my legs, but he presses into my back, pinning my left side to the island. His right foot keeps mine from closing my legs.

"No, no," he murmurs in a silky tone. "You can take it."

My breath hitches, but now I'm determined. He steps away, caressing my hip and steadying me. The spoon taps my wet folds lightly. Each tap sends sparks through my core.

"Gabriel," I breathe.

A cloud of steam billows past me. I've awakened his dragon. He's as excited as I am. I love trying to make him lose control.

"Spank me," I order. "My ass, not my pussy."

"You are not in charge here, my lovely bride," he says, but then he does exactly as I asked, spanking my right and left cheeks with quick, rapid smacks.

"Ouch, ooh." I dance under the onslaught.

He stops and drops the spoon, rubbing away the sting, massaging in the heat. I moan my satisfaction and reach one hand back, seeking him. My fingers close on his shirt, and I use it to pull his body against mine. Well, I try to, anyway. At first he's immovable, obviously needing to control the scene, as always.

But then he steps into me, pressing the bulge of his cock against my ass. "You want me to fuck you here in the kitchen, Tabitha?"

"Yes." There's something so naughty about it that makes it so right.

"Good." He wraps my hair up in his fist and gently tugs my head backward. "Because I think you need to take me deeply right now. Remember who you belong to."

On some level, I'm sure I'm offended, but none of it reaches my brain now. Instead, his words incite more flames of desire, and I let out a little whimper. He gives my ass a slap with his hand, and I turn to watch him unzip and release his erection.

"Show me what you've got, dragon man," I purr,

His lips kick up and pupils slit. "You're too perfect for

words," he breathes, pushing my hair back from my shoulder and scoring my skin with his teeth as he pressed against my entrance.

I reach a hand between my legs to help guide him in.

He shudders the moment he seats himself deep inside me, his breath hot against my cheek. He bands an arm around my waist, creating a cushion between my hip bones at the butcher block, and then starts to shove in rhythmically with deep hard thrusts.

"I like to see you lose control," I tell him, only to regret it because he stops moving.

I shift my hips back to take him deep, and he holds me in tight, caging me with his arm around my hips.

"I don't lose control," he growls against my neck, his open mouth hot and wet against my skin.

"You will." I don't know why I'm taunting him. I guess I just want to interrupt his games. To see the real man behind the expensive suits, perfect hair, and smooth facade. I want the real Gabriel–imperfect, chipped, maybe even a little broken like me.

Until I see that side of him, until he opens up and shows me who he really is, I will keep running. Also until he learns I can't be kept or controlled. I'm not my mother. I won't be bought, caged, or bound by Gabriel Dieter.

"I won't." Thankfully, he starts slowly arcing in and out of me again.

It's tortuously slow, but it feels delicious. Gabriel's smoky scent wraps around me, his searing touch grounds me.

He thrusts harder, pausing at the end of each outstroke, then ramming in and pausing again. It feels like punishment. Like he's teaching me a lesson. What I'm supposed to be learning, I can't say for sure.

That he's in charge. That he won't lose control. That I'm still his prisoner.

None of it is true. I know because his breath grows ragged. He may think he's holding me captive here, but the truth is that I've got him bound. He needs me far more desperately than I want this orgasm. I ultimately hold the upper hand, and I will eventually get my way.

I focus on squeezing my channel around his cock, making his breath quicken even more. Making him pump faster. His thrusts shake the butcher block. A vase tips, spilling flowers and water.

We both ignore the mess. We're too close now. It feels too glorious to stop or slow down. I let him hear my desire in my throaty cries, the way I roll my hips back to meet his.

Steam clouds my vision. The room fills with a smoky scent. From him?

Must be.

Our exhales twine together in time with his thrusts. My eyes roll back in my head, and my legs start to shake. My orgasm looms, bright and yellow and shimmering with a pulsing red.

"Tabitha." More steam billows past my face. "Tabitha."

Gabriel pulls out, shifting the arm around my waist, so he can cup between my legs. He shoves several fingers in a cone inside me, and I come all over them at the same time he shoots his load across my ass. His cum is deliciously hot and thick.

I shake and squeeze his fingers in spasms of my release.

I've never been a fan of the pull-out method, and not because it's unreliable in preventing pregnancy. There's something just not satisfying about finishing alone.

"Are you afraid I'll get pregnant?" I ask. Maybe he

doesn't know there are other methods of birth control in the twenty-first century.

"What?" He shifts his hand to rub my clit, and I come again, bucking my hips against the butcher block.

"Is that why you don't come inside me?"

He draws in a sharp breath and tucks his cock away, somehow managing to look put together and business-like after what we just did. "No. One day, I will breed you."

Oh god. Mini orgasm. I don't even want kids but something about stern dragon daddy making it sound like I don't have a choice? *Hot.* "Kinda hard to do that when you don't cum inside me." I force my voice to remain light and level. "Unless you missed that medieval health class." I'll explain about my birth control implant later.

He glowers at me under his thick brows.

"You're holding back," I say, and my voice hitches despite my efforts. "Please tell me why."

He reaches for me once more, pulling my back against his front and cupping my breast with one hand, my pussy with the other. An effective way of avoiding my probing, but I'll let him distract me.

A few more rubs and my head falls back against his shoulder.

"That's it," he murmurs, and his rasping voice in my ear makes my arousal spiral higher. "Give over control." Another aftershock runs through me. Gabriel plays my body like a musician plays an instrument, seeming to know how to hit every note with perfect clarity. Putting them together to make a symphony of sensations that are like none I've ever felt before.

"I don't understand…" I pant. My brain is soup. "I've never been able to…" I trail off, not willing to finish the sentence, but Gabriel has caught on.

"Tell me."

I lick my lips. I've never come like this with anyone. My previous sexual encounters were so forgettable it's laughable. If the guy could fumble around and even find my clit, he wouldn't know what to do with it. Gabriel works my body like he knows every inch, like he's designed it, studied every angle and curve. He could pull me apart and put me back together. "I've never been with someone where I've shared such explosive chemistry," I hedge. "Especially not someone who is someone my mother would approve of."

"Your mother would approve of me?" He lets me turn to face him.

"Oh yes." I tick off on my fingers, "Well-dressed, handsome, obviously ultra-wealthy, owns a castle. She would nag me to make sure I stay on your good side. She'd book me waxing appointments and buy me racy lingerie, so I could *keep you happy.*"

"I see." His eyes narrow. "But what about you, Tabitha? Am I your type?"

"Well." I kind of like that he's not asking about my mother anymore, but he's trying to get me to open up when he won't even answer my questions. "No, not really." *Except in looks and in the sack.* "I tend to run away from guys like you. Rich, powerful, overbearing. I had too much of men like that growing up. It's my mom's type."

"What sort of man would you prefer?"

"Does it matter? Would you change for me?"

"I am capable of change."

I wrinkle my nose. Do I want Gabriel to be more like the men I've dated? Those guys were all free spirits, like me. Vagabonds with no jobs or roots. In Taos, they're the Trustafarians who've given themselves new names and smoke a lot of pot and talk about "finding themselves." I felt comfortable with them. But we were like jellyfish, drifting through life.

Gabriel isn't a jellyfish. He's a dragon. An intense, powerful, obnoxiously controlling, and obsessive dragon. There's no comparison.

Compared to Gabriel, sex with the guys I dated is like drinking dirty brackish water versus rich fine wine. Which is probably why I've only had a handful of hookups. I thought I just wasn't into long-term relationships, but maybe I wasn't choosing guys I wanted to be with. I was scratching an itch and moving on.

Gabriel...he could consume my world. I could become obsessed with him. And that's exactly what he wants. A shiver runs through me.

I hope he won't notice, but he's completely in tune with me, as I'm in tune with him.

"I can't compare you with those guys. Being with you is so much more satisfying," I admit. "On another level."

"And that is why you are so eager to leave me?"

My insides churn, and I give him a desperate look.

"Ah yes," he caresses my face. "You are afraid of what we share."

"Love is control."

"Ah, but, Tabitha, control sets you free."

I lift my wrists. "Take these trackers off, and we can have a conversation about control."

He presses his lips together.

"That's what I thought." I plant a hand on his chest and push him out of my way, wanting a cloth to clean myself with. I'm naked and Gabriel is still fully clothed. Again.

I grab the robe and yank it on. "I'm going to keep trying to escape."

"You cannot run from me. I will not allow it." He grips my wrist just above the golden cuff. His fist tightens. "I cannot allow you to be hurt again."

Again? For a moment, I have a clear vision of the tapestry I stumbled upon in the dusty area of the castle. The one with the woman with long brown hair. *She looks a little like me.*

"In the interest of change," he spits it like a dirty word, "and making you happy, I propose a compromise."

"What?" This is new.

Gabriel's dark brows knot together. "Don't misunderstand. My preference is to keep you in a cage. To keep you on your back or pregnant for the next ten years."

My pussy clenches even as my mind rebels.

His lips curl. He moves me in front of him, sliding his hand around me, pressing his palm to my belly as he rasps in my ear, "I still could. Put you in the cage while I work, let you out only at night. Carry you to my bed, feed you…" Smoke rolls down my cheek. His hard cock probes my bottom. "You'd like it, Tabitha. A part of you would thrive."

I push away and face him. "And a part of me would die."

"Yes." He sounds sad. "So I propose a compromise. Forty days and forty nights as my bride. You remain at my side and obey my commands. After that, if you wish to leave, I will let you go."

"No way."

"Forty days and forty nights. The number of days the Nazarene wandered in the desert."

"Or like the trial period for WinRAR."

My lips twitch at Gabriel's perplexed look.

"It's a file archiving software." I consider him. "How do I know you're not going to renege?"

"My word is my bond."

"All right, then." Forty days and forty nights aren't so bad. I get to live out my princess in the castle dreams and then bail. "*A three-hour tour*," I sing and make a face when his face remains blank. "Come on, you don't know Gilligan's Island? I need to work on your modern education, so you get my references. Let's put that on the to-do list."

A trace of indulgence settles on Gabriel's face, the tension leaving his jaw. He's relieved that I've agreed to stay, even for the limited duration.

"But I need to contact my friends. And my mom. They need to know I'm all right."

"You earn the right to call your friends when I feel I can trust you. I will not have you giving those wolves the location of my castle."

"What about an email?"

"I will consider an email."

"Fine. I'll take it. Though an email from me would raise more red flags in my friend's minds than a text or call…"

"There will be no texts or calls, Tabitha." He lowers his voice. "Perhaps I should keep you in the cage for the duration of our bargain."

"That wasn't the agreement," I say, but my inner thighs squeeze together, reacting to the threat as if he just promised me pleasure.

He dips his head close. "You'd like that, wouldn't you?" he murmurs. "Being locked in the cage while I work. Naked and at my mercy."

"No," I croak. I'm lying. My core throbs like he's stroked my clit.

"Are you sure? I could tie you up with a toy between your legs. I'd take breaks often to give you…relief. If you're good. And punish you if you've been bad."

"That sounds awful." That sounds great. I squirm, impossibly turned on. "Is it hot in here?"

His dark chuckle sends thrills up my spine. "You love it

when I force you to obey me. I could keep you like this forever. You'd spend your days locked in the cage and your nights cuffed to my bed. Eventually, you'd forget what it was like to be free."

I swallow. "You promised."

"Yes, I promised. My word is good. But for the next forty days and forty nights…you are mine."

9

Gabriel

I SWOOP Tabitha into my arms and carry her in the direction of her chamber.

"Where are we going?"

"To your chamber."

She kicks her pretty feet. "Nope. Not happening. We just made a deal."

"I wanted you naked in that bedroom waiting for me when I got off work. I wanted to think of you lying on the bed, bare, ready, and impatient for me."

Her laugh is throaty. "You're ridiculous, dragon. The most ridiculous man I've ever known."

Do I detect traces of affection in her tone? Certainly, it's there in the way her arms twine loosely about my neck. She's comfortable in my arms, being carried by me.

"I can't have you running about my castle naked. That is not acceptable."

"I'm not naked, I'm in your robe. Which is quite

comfortable, by the way. But if you want me in clothes, you'll have to give me back my wardrobe. There's no more locking me in the bedroom. We made a deal."

"I've already told you that caging you is within my rights."

"You have no right to me, dragon."

We've reached her bedroom, and I stride over to the bed. "I have every right." I toss her on the bed and climb over her.

She laughs like it's all quite amusing to her. She doesn't realize it's the truth.

"I'm your mate, little human. That makes me your keeper. Your protector. Your punisher. And your provider."

"Am I supposed to swoon over those words? Because I find them a bit lacking in the poetry department."

"You're supposed to swoon over this," I tell her, pushing her knees wide and settling between her legs. I lick into her, parting her ripe flesh with my tongue.

"Mmm. Oh," she pants, but she pushes my head away. "Wait, wait. Wait, Gabriel."

"What is it, my treasure?"

She pushes herself up on her elbows. "Is this your plan?"

I arch a brow.

"Give me orgasms morning, noon, and night for forty days? Is that how you plan to convince me to stay?"

I blink at her. "Is it working?"

"No," she lies, rubbing her lips together. I want to kiss them, but I don't trust myself not to lose control.

"What would work, my treasure?"

"I want an end to the secrets and the riddles and the games. I want to know the real you."

"Games are who I am. They are what I love."

She shakes her head. "No. Games are what you hide behind."

My brows drop. I can't decipher what it is she wants from me. I can't read into this. I'm at a total loss.

A flash of chilly desperation ices my chest. What if… there is nothing else to me? This person she seeks doesn't exist?

"There!" she pokes a darling finger into my chest. "What are you thinking right now?"

My mind goes blank. "I beg your pardon?"

"What were you thinking? What made you frown? I want to know what's going on in your head—no, not your head. Your heart."

My…heart?

"You want to know what's going on in my heart?"

"Yes."

I take her hand and hold it to my chest, where the organ in question lies. "There are many who would tell you I have no heart, Tabitha. But it's not true. I do have one, but it only beats for you. You brought me out of my slumber. I lived only to meet you again, and now you've come to me. I have lived hundreds of years without you. Far too many. So please, you must forgive me if I do not even know what it's like to live with a heart because I've only just come alive again."

Curses.

I've said too much. I've frightened her again. Her jade eyes round with concern.

But Tabitha reaches out and traces the lines of my cheek, then along my jaw. "Hearts can be a lot to manage," she murmurs.

"Yes."

"Are you having a hard time managing yours?"

A rush of emotion flushes through me. It's unfamiliar,

both in quantity and tone. I hardly understand it. "Yes." My voice rasps in my throat. It's the most honest I've been with her.

"Come here," she murmurs, wrapping her slender arms behind my neck again, drawing me down on top of her. "I'll show you how it's done."

And then she kisses me. Her lips are infinitely soft. A gentle exploration. She moves them across mine a few times, then slips her tongue between mine.

All the while, I keep my mouth perfectly still. Afraid to move. To kiss her back. To claim her gorgeous mouth the way I'm dying to.

"Kiss me," she whispers against my lips. Her eyelids flutter.

She's so beautiful. So frightfully lovely. She's starlight and sunshine and laughter. She's spring flowers and a baby's sweet babble.

My dragon thrashes within me. I force myself to move slowly. I cage her head between both my hands and drink from her lips, inhaling at the same time to take in her spring rain and honeysuckle scent.

And...nothing terrible happens.

I don't breathe fire in her face and destroy the one thing in this world I love. I don't even feel the urge to claim her. The kiss was tender. Sweet. A gift to my bride. The dragon remains quiet, as if it's enough for him, too.

I slowly draw away, and Tabitha smiles. "That was nice."

My cock lengthens along my pant leg, but I ignore it.

"Was that what you needed, Tabitha?"

"Yes."

"I think I understand." I do, and I don't. I understand the essence of it but not how to go about it.

"I want my clothes back," Tabitha says.

I smirk. "I'll have them brought in, my treasure. You like them?"

"Yes." She blushes a bit. "Designer clothes are my guilty pleasure. I like to make my own, and I love to vintage shop, but sometimes nothing beats a good pair of Dior shoes, you know?"

I run my thumb over her lower lip. "May I take you shopping? We could hit Paris and Milan to find you a gown for the Christmas ball. Maybe ring in the new year somewhere special?"

I expect a surge of rage from my dragon at the idea of letting her leave the castle before she's been fire-branded, but I don't sense anything. Of course, he was the one who showed her how to escape. I can't begin to unpack that.

Tabitha sits up, her face alight. "Ooh, that sounds fun!"

Finally, a way to impress her.

I drop a kiss on her forehead. "I'll call the pilot and have him prepare the jet. And I'll have your clothes returned, so you can pack."

She climbs to her feet on the bed and bounces up and down. "We're going shopping!"

My chest fills with a dizzying warmth. I've finally pleased my mate in a non-sexual way. I ignore all the misgivings I have about her using the trip to escape. We came to an agreement.

Surely she will honor her end.

~

Tabitha

I come out of the shower with a towel wrapped around my hair to find Gabriel lounging on the bed with a neatly packed suitcase open on the bed, and my closets returned to their former glory.

"How do you make things happen so fast?" I wonder aloud.

"I have many tricks," he tells me. His lids lower to half-mast as his gaze roams across my naked body. I pull the towel off my head and shake my wet hair out over my shoulders, feeling sexier than I ever did in all my years as a model.

"When are we leaving?"

Gabriel lifts his elegant shoulders. "Take your time, my treasure. Whenever you are ready, we'll get on the plane. My pilot flies on our schedule."

"Wow. But we're going tonight? Right now? As soon as I'm ready?"

Of all the mind-reeling things that have happened since I woke in this castle, it's funny that leaving for Paris on short notice is the one that seems hardest to believe.

I mean… dragons.

That one should've blown my head right off my shoulders.

Yet somehow it came easily. Maybe because I'd already learned about werewolves. Maybe because of the dream. For some reason, it just made sense. Gabriel is a dragon. It explains his eccentricities. Excuses his insanities. Not that it means I'm staying.

I'm not.

I mean, not without him…

My brain spins out on what it would take for me to stay with Gabriel after the forty days and forty nights have passed.

He'd have to show me more of himself. He'd have to give up control–be more of a free spirit like me. And I'd want more kisses.

Maybe that's why I'm so excited about this Paris trip. I have a wanderlust that needs to be slaked. The fact that

ALPHA'S FIRE

Gabriel suggested it spontaneously and then arranged it in a matter of minutes thrills me.

I mean, he does have a private jet. I don't care about luxury, but the convenience is pretty cool.

I pull on a soft cropped sweater and a pair of Gucci jeans with high-heeled boots and a matching belt. I love clothes but haven't worn full-on designer like this since my years as a model. It feels fun in a way it never did then.

I take my time in the bathroom, blowing my hair dry and applying makeup and then I come out, throw my arms wide and announce, "I'm ready." I drop the cosmetic bag into the suitcase and zip it closed.

"You're magnificent," Gabriel murmurs, rising from where he was lounging on my bed and picking up the suitcase at the same time he holds out a hand.

I take his hand. My pulse picks up speed at his pleasure. We had a rocky start, but now that we've struck an accord, it feels like we're dating. And I'm actually excited by my date, for the first time ever.

He finds a cashmere coat for me in the closet and wraps it around my shoulders, then carries the bag (even though it has wheels) and ushers me out of the room.

We travel in an elevator to some lower level–lower than the evil villain warehouse with the cage–and when we exit, we're in some kind of giant hangar filled with rows and rows of luxury cars. Lamborghinis, Porsches, Teslas, a Bentley, a pearl gray Aston Martin.

Am I impressed? Okay, maybe a little. Only because they are beautiful and sexy. Not because a man with a big bank account turns me on.

Gabriel leads me to a Learjet where a uniformed pilot stands at the ready. They converse in Italian, and then we board the jet, and the pilot backs it out of the hangar.

"My mom would be so impressed," I tell Gabriel when

he shows me to my seat, and an attendant offers me a glass of champagne.

He reaches over to buckle my seatbelt like I'm a child. I would take offense, but after seeing how he melted down about me being in danger on the cliff wall, I understand how terrified he is of me getting hurt. "But not you?"

I shrug. "Money isn't everything."

"But it's not something to disdain, is it, my treasure? Will you refuse the gifts I want to shower you with?"

I lift my chin. "I won't trade my freedom for your gold."

Gabriel studies me. "That is what happened with your mother." It's a statement, not a question.

I nod.

"What happened?"

I sigh. "The same thing happened over and over again. My mom would work hard to land a rich man. He would take us in. Provide things. My mother provided him with things. He would get controlling. Make demands. Eventually, things would blow up, and she'd be off looking for the new man."

"You judge her for this."

Gabriel's statement takes my breath away. Not in a good way. More like a sucker punch. Am I judging my mom? I don't think of it that way, but perhaps I am.

"I don't want to be like her," I say, but I sound a little defensive. I don't think of myself as a judgmental person. I frown, considering my feelings toward my mom's behavior a little more. "I guess..." I say slowly, "I guess I could always feel my mom's fear. It's like she was always scrambling for the money, even though we didn't need that kind of luxury. There was always a whiff of desperation to her, and that's what led her to accept these less than ideal relationships."

Gabriel takes my hand as the jet starts down a runway. "She never saved any of the money? Invested it?" The jet lifts off the ground. I wonder if it feels unnatural for Gabriel to fly in a jet when he's capable of flying with his own wings. Or maybe he enjoys flying, no matter how.

"Never. This is so sad, but she never profited from any of the relationships. She never had her own money. She was married three times, but always with a prenup that left her with nothing if they divorced. And they always divorced."

"What about your father? He did not provide for you?" Gabriel's growl has an edge to it on my behalf.

I shrug. "He died from a car accident before I was born, leaving my mom with a heap of medical bills and a baby on the way."

"And now she is with a stockbroker in Scottsdale."

"You've done your homework. Yes, a grumpy, rigid stockbroker who is loaded and tells her what she can and can't do."

"Perhaps she likes giving up control?" Gabriel suggests with a subtle flick of his brows. As if he thinks I like giving up control.

I don't.

I mean...well, only in bed. But that's different.

"No. It bothered her. I think that's why it bothers me. So I decided at a pretty young age I would never go that route. Money and nice things just aren't that important to me. Since you've clearly researched me, you probably know I live in a train car. It's *tres* boho chic."

Gabriel's lips quirk. "I've seen your little train car, Tabitha. It's as unique and charming as you."

Unique and charming is one way to put it. My mom thinks it's filled with junk. "You liked it? I restored it and decorated it all myself."

"That is obvious. It is completely to your taste. I loved it. I love everything about you, my treasure."

I'm ridiculously gratified by his reaction. I supposed I imagined he'd pooh-poohed my lifestyle like all my mother's boyfriends do.

"Would you live there with me?" It's a challenge. I want to know what he'll say. He thinks I'm his mate—would he flex for me? Or does he just expect me to leave everything I was to be his dragon-bride?

"I would be enchanted. Although my dragon prefers space. It might be difficult for me to spend a lengthy amount of time in such a confined area."

"I get that. I also like my space—I can't deal with crowds. People's energies, emotions, their auras, it gets to be too much." I flick my hands like I'm clearing the air around my head.

"Is that why you wander?" He seems genuinely interested.

"Yeah. My close friends expect me to disappear for a month at a time. I need the silence, the solitude, the emptiness to recalibrate. To breathe. But…Taos is home." I pause, digesting what he said. "You would come? To Taos? You'd live with me?" To say I'm shocked would be an understatement.

"Certainly. You have friends there. Friends who are like family to you. That is why I will not harm your wolves despite their wishes to harm me."

I'm almost winded by the sudden constriction in my chest. "They wish to harm you?" I shouldn't be afraid for Gabriel. He's a dragon. He breathes fire. But the thought of anything happening to him sends inexplicable bolts of fear through my entire body.

"Do not fear, Tabitha," Gabriel says with a casual wave of his hand. "I can handle your wolves."

"Why do they want to harm you?"

"Their government sent them to spy on me, and I returned fire. It is a cat and mouse game, nothing more." His gaze is warm on my face. He reaches out and strokes his thumb down my cheek. "Were you worried for me or for them?"

I swallow. "For both of you." It's not a lie, but it's an obfuscation of the truth. It was Gabriel's safety that concerned me the most. A fact that makes me feel guilty now.

"When can we go to Taos?" I ask. The sooner I can get in touch with my friends, the better, for so many reasons–the most primary one being my freedom.

"After I've claimed you." His lids droop like the idea of claiming me turns him on. We've reached final altitude, and the jet straightens out. The sky is a clear, thin blue.

"Does that mean marry me?"

"Yes."

For some reason, I feel like he's leaving something out. Like claiming means more than marriage, but he says nothing more, just watches me with that glittering gaze of his.

"I don't know if I believe you, Gabriel."

"I would never lie to you, my treasure."

10

Gabriel

"This is the one." Tabitha spins around in a strapless Carolina Herrera gown in burgundy, red, and gold. It has a short skirt but a long train in the back and a giant bow at the front at her waist.

"Only someone with a figure like yours can pull this gown off," our private stylist says in a melodious French accent. "It's one of those gowns designed for models not the general public."

Tabitha shoots me a look under her long lashes. "The colors are right, aren't they, Gabriel?"

I have to rub my face to cover the steam that streams from my nostrils. The need to claim Tabitha has been coming on even harder since we've been in Paris. I made it through the past two nights, but my dragon grows more and more restless.

Right now, seeing her in our colors drives me mad with desire.

"You look spectacular." To the stylist, I say, "We'll take it."

"Wonderful, do you need shoes to match?"

"Yes, what do you have?" Tabitha asks.

"Let me bring you some options. What is your size?"

"I wear an eight in US sizing, which is 39 in European."

The stylist disappears, and Tabitha twirls for me again, swishing the train like a dragon's tail.

"You're incredible." My voice is gruff with desire.

She struts over and rips off my sunglasses. Her wide smile is triumphant when she sees my dragon eyes. "You love seeing me in your colors."

"I do," I admit. I also love that she's enjoying herself.

Tabitha has been at ease since we arrived in Paris two nights ago. She's enjoyed shopping and sightseeing. She hasn't tried to escape or use a phone although I did allow her to email her friends last night. I couldn't risk her speaking to them. Not yet.

But soon, I hope, my bride will accept me.

In the meantime, I must do everything I can to stay in control. Which, unfortunately, is getting harder by the minute. Especially when I'm confined in a large city without any space to shift and fly.

But tonight is New Year's Eve. I've arranged a private, romantic dinner in the finest restaurant in Paris. I can't risk crowds or anything that would set my dragon off with jealousy or fear for her safety. Now that she's found the dress she loves, we can return to Romania tomorrow.

The stylist returns, and Tabitha quickly thrusts my sunglasses back on my face.

"I found several really nice options that would complement the dress."

"Ruby slippers!" Tabitha exclaims as if that should mean something to me. "No?" She puts them on and clicks her heels. "Let's see if they work." She closes her eyes. "There's no place like home. There's no place like home."

It's some cultural reference I slept through, but judging by the way the stylist stares at Tabitha, equally mystified, I suspect it's an American one.

"It's an old movie, no?" the stylist asks.

Tabitha slips the shoes off and tries on a pair of red stilettos. "Yes. *The Wizard of Oz*. It was written as an allegory of American politics during the turn of the century. Most people don't know that, though. They think it's a family movie."

I watch Tabitha slip her feet into a pair of golden high-heeled sandals, allowing the stylist to buckle the slender gold straps around her ankles. She may have been living in a train car, but she's as regal as any queen in any century. My bride was born to rule at my side.

"We really need to work on your pop culture references, Gabriel." She looks at the stylist. "He's the only one on the planet who hasn't watched *Friends*. I almost want him to avoid it. Remain pure."

The stylist laughs. "Even I have watched *Friends*." She sits back and surveys Tabitha. "These are your shoes, no? They look perfect."

"They do, but I sort of want the ruby slippers."

"We'll take both," I cut in. She should have anything her heart desires.

"Are you getting impatient?" There's laughter in Tabitha's expression.

"Never, my treasure. I could watch you try on clothes all day."

"You *have* watched me try on clothes all day," she reminds me. "Yesterday, too. And you bought almost everything I tried on."

"I want you to have everything you enjoy."

"I enjoy Taos," she says pointedly, stepping out of the unbuckled sandals and turning to give her back to the stylist, who helps her unzip the elaborate gown. "I enjoy my friends. I enjoy calling my mother on New Year's to wish her a happy holiday. Especially when I missed calling her on Christmas because someone was flying me across the ocean!"

My dick goes rock hard when the dress comes off, and my beautiful mate stands in the private dressing room in nothing but a tiny G-string. But we're not alone, and my dragon is unstable.

I need to get her back to my penthouse where I can ravish her before dinner.

"We'll call your mother before dinner," I tell her because my desire to please my bride overrides my usual need to control the situation and her.

"Really?" she brightens, picking up her bra and putting it on, then donning the sweater dress she arrived in.

"I want to meet this woman who will be in my court when it comes to convincing you to marry me."

Tabitha pulls on her calfskin boots and wraps a matching belt around her hips. "If you think my mother has any influence whatsoever over my love life, you are sorely mistaken."

I love the teasing lilt to her voice. There's a playfulness, a lightness between us that has been here from the beginning. It's all Tabitha. She is lightness and laughter. Pleasure and kindness.

"Oh, I haven't underestimated the challenge you will give me, Tabitha." I catch her gaze and hold it, loving the way her breath hitches and her pulse thrums at her neck. I hold out my hand. "Come, beautiful. I need to be the one who undresses you next time."

Tabitha

Gabriel sits on the bed with me between his knees, my back to his front. He holds a tablet in front of me, ready to video conference my mom.

We're in a stunning penthouse in Paris–another property owned by Gabriel. I've been in a lot of luxurious surroundings, thanks to my mother's obsession with men who have money, but this has amenities I never even knew existed. Unlike the castle in Romania, the decor here is all ultra-modern. It features cool colors, sleek lines, and high-tech conveniences.

The bathtub is made of white quartz streaked with purples and black, and the floor is heated, so when you get out, you never touch cold tile. The towels also are warmed on a towel rack.

The bed appears to float over the floor although it's an architectural illusion. The wall-to-wall windows look out over the cathedral of Montmartre. A flight of stairs leads to a rooftop patio with natural gas fire tables and torches, so that even now in winter, it's quite comfortable to lounge on the plush outdoor furniture and sip champagne between rounds of sex.

"Remember the rules, my treasure. Our deal is off if you break them."

I elbow Gabriel in the ribs. "Don't be an ass, Gabriel. I already agreed to the rules." The rules were not to mention where we are nor the location of his castle. Not to try to get any secret messages across to my mother.

I don't feel the need to. For one thing, I know my mother will be too caught up in her own dramas to even pick up on a secret message if I tried to give her one. But I also feel safe enough with Gabriel. I trust he will honor our agreement. I may be his prisoner, but it's not permanent. It's the only way a possessive, old-fashioned dragon knew how to court me. I don't love it, but I understand.

Besides, I'm starting to really enjoy my time with Gabriel. Right now, my body is languid with the multiple orgasms he gave me when we returned from our shopping spree. That was after he'd spent a solid two hours this morning worshiping my body before we left. But more than that, now that he's opened up a little and I've seen what he hides beneath the slick surface, I feel I can trust him.

I hope so, anyway.

He nibbles on my neck. "Forgive me," he murmurs against my skin. "I'm afraid of losing you."

There he goes again. Opening up. I think he realized that showing me how much I matter to him softened me.

He hits call on the tablet, and it rings my mother. He has somehow signed in as me on the iPad, even though I never gave him my login information. It's still early in the day in the United States. My mom should answer.

"Tabitha!" Her face looms close, then she pulls back as she realizes we're connected. "How are you, my darling? I've missed hearing from you. You know I hate when you go—oh!" She catches sight of Gabriel when he shifts the screen slightly and stops with her mouth agape. "Who is this?"

"This is Gabriel. The man I'm..." *Being held prisoner by. Supposedly fated to mate. Having mad, wild orgasms with.* "...seeing."

"You cannot be her mother. Sisters, surely," Gabriel says, his charm and charisma turned to full blast. Just the sound of that sexy, suave voice makes my thighs snap together to alleviate the ache between my legs.

My mother loves it, of course. "You're too sweet. I'm Celeste."

"I see where your daughter gets her beauty."

My mother flutters her eyelashes and waves her hand. "So, where did you meet? What do you do? You don't look like the usual Taos resident."

"You're right, I'm not from Taos, but Tabitha has persuaded me to spend more time there."

I shoot a surprised glance at him over my shoulder. He had told me he would go, but the conversation felt more theoretical. He says it now like it's been decided. We'll be together, and he'll spend time in Taos with me.

I'm shocked by how appealing I find the idea. Could it be that I no longer wish to return home alone?

"What do you do, Gabriel?"

It's always an important question for my mom to ask handsome men.

"A bit of everything," he answers.

"Gabriel is independently wealthy," I fill in. "I don't think he needs to do anything unless he wants to."

I expect my mother's instant approval, and she doesn't disappoint. Her eyes light with interest. "Well then, take good care of my daughter," she instructs him.

Huh. I expected her to tell me to take good care of him.

"Speaking of which, darling, I have some wonderful news."

I push away from Gabriel, wanting to give my mom some privacy for her wonderful news, but he catches me around the waist and pulls me back. Of course, he wants to monitor my every word.

Grr.

I angle the tablet, so his face doesn't show in the window. "What is it?"

"I've come into some money of my own. A great deal. I can help you buy a real house now, and set you up with a trust fund, so you don't have to vagabond about the country antiquing."

I open my mouth to argue with her about the vagabonding remark but then close it again as something hits me.

"Where did the money come from, Mom?"

"Well... I'm trying to figure that out. It was a gift from one of my past admirers, I just can't determine which one. I don't know whether he died and left it in a will or what happened, exactly. I received a letter from the lawyer, and then the funds were in my account the next day. *Thirty million!*" She whispers the last two words.

A flush of awareness comes over me. I want to giggle and burst into tears at the same time. I have a strong suspicion about where that money came from.

"Wow, Mom. What are you going to do with it?"

"Well, I'm leaving James, for one thing," she says. "I'm tired of him dangling money over my head as a means to control me."

I suck in my breath. Tears stab my eyes. "That's great." My voice wobbles. "I guess your next relationship can be on your own terms."

"That's right, darling. So can yours." She looks at me pointedly. "All I ever wanted was to give you a life of ease and luxury. Now I can finally do it."

My God. Was my mother contorting herself into terrible relationships all these years believing she was doing it *for me?*

How absolutely tragic.

Two tears streak down my cheeks. "Mom, I didn't need that," I say. "Ease and luxury are overrated. Happiness isn't. Personal fulfillment isn't. Loving relationships aren't."

My mom waves her hand again, not noticing that I'm crying. "I know you think so, darling, but I wanted to provide. I wanted you to be provided for. I want my grandchildren to have a charmed existence."

"They certainly will," Gabriel murmurs for my ears only, his lips soft against my shoulder. His fingers stroke lightly up and down across my belly.

"So you don't think I need to land a wealthy man anymore?" I try to keep my voice light, but I'm still a little choked up.

"You should look for that happiness, Tabitha. Love and your personal fulfillment. You've got a wealthy mom now."

I let out a watery laugh. "That's great, Mom. I'm so happy for you."

"I love you, darling."

"I love you, too. Happy new year."

"Happy new year. Let me see that handsome date of yours again."

I shift the screen, so Gabriel's face comes into view.

"Be good to my daughter. She deserves it," she says.

"I worship the ground she walks on," Gabriel swears.

I let out a scoff, and he nips my shoulder.

"Bye, Mom."

"Happy new year, Celeste," Gabriel says and ends the call.

I stand and turn to face him. "You did that, didn't you?"

"What, my treasure?" His expression is smooth and impassive.

"The money. Did you set my mother up because of what I told you?"

He inclines his head. "Your mother need not worry about money ever again."

Fresh tears pop into my eyes. "You know you shot yourself in the foot, right? Because now she's no longer in the *Marry Tabitha off to a rich man* camp?"

Gabriel's large palms settle at my waist. "I didn't think she was going to be the vote that swayed you, anyway," he says softly. His gaze is warm and gentle. He reaches up to thumb away a tear.

I fall into him, wrapping my arms around his neck and straddling his waist with my knees bent. "You didn't have to do that."

"Of course I did. She's my family now." He nuzzles in the open neckline of my robe, kissing it open until he reaches my breast.

"You're pretty damn sure of yourself, aren't you, dragon?"

He sucks one nipple into his mouth. It's already sore and chafed from his previous attentions, but that doesn't stop the zing of excitement from traveling straight to my ready core.

"I can't fail at winning you, Tabitha."

You won't, I almost tell him. But I'm not ready to concede defeat yet. If it's really a defeat. I'm beginning to think it might be a win-win. The happily ever after I always believed in, I just thought it wouldn't be with the prince, but the pauper.

I pull back and cup his face. "Thank you. It means a lot to my mom, and that means something to me."

"I know, my treasure. Don't worry. I will always take care of the people who you love. Even those wolves of yours."

"I don't think they need you to take care of them. They do a decent job of that themselves."

"I just mean I won't harm them. They were my adversaries, but I won't destroy them."

Oh. Wow. I'm a little disturbed by his words, but then, I suspected Gabriel was dangerous.

"Do you... harm many people?" I have to ask. I mean, I can't just settle down with the villain, no matter how kind he may be to me.

"Not the innocent, no." But his gaze grows distant and a haunted quality comes over his face. "Except by accident."

I remember the gold cuffs I saw on his dragon in the vision.

"Your dragon is dangerous."

His gaze snaps to mine, and his expression smooths. He lifts me by my waist to set me on my feet. "We should get ready for dinner, little human."

"So I'm right," I persist, but he's already up, walking away, a phone at his ear. It was a question he didn't want to answer.

I should be frightened to hear he can't always control the animal side of him, but I'm not. For some reason, I feel a huge surge of sympathy for the dragon.

He can't help what he is.

Or how dangerous he can be.

And then I'm sorry for Gabriel, too. He seems so together, so controlled, but it's for good reason. He has a dark side that could lay waste to an entire countryside with one angry bellow of fire.

How lonely it must be for him—to be this relic from the past, a beast he must keep from all those around him for fear they will be harmed.

All the more reason for me to stay.

Gabriel Dieter—man and dragon—needs me.

11

Rafe

"I dunno, Sarge. This is a shit lead," Channing mutters.

We're huddled in a dark corner, waiting in the freezing rain. There are few people out on the Parisian streets. The only movement comes from a few patrons ducking into a dark doorway lit by a neon sign.

Channing looks like a wannabe rapper in baggy jeans, seven hundred dollar sneakers, and a bright, brand-name shirt. Club attire, so he can blend in if need be.

Deke is a silent shadow at my side. He and I are dressed for combat. It's just the three of us. Lance is back in Taos, holding down the homefront and guarding our mates.

"It's all we got," I tell Channing. "But it's a good lead. You weren't there when I got my ear chewed off by the Tucson Alpha. His mate had a vision when she held something Tabitha made. She saw fire."

"That can mean a lot of things," Channing says.

"Not according to her. The fire and Tabitha were inextricably linked. Like a bond. Like a mate. And who do we know who breathes fire and has been searching for his mate?"

"Gabriel Dieter," Deke growls.

"I fucking hate him," Channing says.

"Yeah, join the club," I say. "Gabriel Dieter's gone to ground. No movement at any of his known headquarters. He's got Tabitha, I know it." My breath puffs in the cold air. "This is our only lead."

"Well, at least we know if he has her, it means she's safe. Physically, at least. He wouldn't harm his own mate," Deke reasons.

"True," I say. "But the guy loves to play games. Who knows what kind of psychological bullshit he's pulling on her right now. And I seriously doubt she's with him consensually."

"What about the email?" Channing asks.

Deke growls. "That email is bullshit. Sadie says Tabitha never emails when she could call, and never calls when she could text."

"Fine. When do I go in?" Channing nods at the club's neon sign. "Not that I'm complaining about waiting out in the rain. It's just I went through all this trouble to find this swag outfit, I want to show it off." He grins at his orange trainers. They're such a bright color, they glow in the dark.

Deke narrows his eyes at Channing. "You look…"

"Awesome? Epic? On fleek?" Channing hums a party anthem and shuffles his feet in a poor imitation of a moonwalk.

Deke tilts his head. "Nope. You look wrong. Just…wrong."

Channing stops dancing. "I do not! This outfit is steezy. I got the drip."

"Yeah, no." Deke leans out of the rain, the picture of a bored wolf picking a fight. "More like cheugy."

"What does that even mean—"

"Quiet." I raise a hand, and their argument cuts out. "That's our target."

A rangy young man with a shock of dyed red hair has stepped out of the club. He saunters through the rain, steam rising from his jacket, and leans against the graffiti-covered wall.

I flick my fingers, giving the signal. We can't risk talking because our target's a shifter. Channing nods and starts across the street towards the club. Deke disappears into the night.

I wait a beat and follow Channing, cutting left while he heads right. He stands between the club door and the alley where the redhead is lighting up.

I can tell the target's a dragon shifter because he lights the end of his cigarette with a flick of his fingers.

I hunch in my coat like I'm hurrying against the winter wind and enter the alley.

The redhead straightens, sensing danger. His eyes flare red.

I hold up my hands. No sense going up armed against a dragon. Not when he can transform and breathe fire. "I just want to talk," I say in English and repeat the phrase in French.

The redhead wheels from the wall, turning to run in the opposite direction.

Deke falls from the roof of the club, cutting off his escape. Now the target is pinned between me and Deke, with Channing standing guard at the mouth of the alley.

There's a shout and a flare of heat behind me. I duck. A ball of fire blazes over my head, barely missing Deke. He ducks to tackle the redhead.

Channing drags a second dark-haired dragon shifter into the alley. I help hold him down and cuff him. The dragon struggles. Sparks fly from his fingers, but the second the silver cuffs are on him the flames snuff out. Nothing but smoke.

"No more fireballs, asshole." Channing shoves the dark-haired shifter's shoulder.

"Fucking dogs," the shifter on the pavement says. His accent is more English than French. We pull him to his feet. He has the same pale, freckled face as his brother.

"There's two of them," Channing says.

"Gemini dragons." I turn. Deke has the redhead by the collar, both of them looking towards the first dragon shifter's brother. The redhead isn't resisting now that we have his brother. It's a standoff.

"You British?" Channing asks.

"Fuck no," both the brothers say. Mentally I name the red-head Castor and his brother, Pollux.

Pollux sneers., "We're Welsh."

"Enough." I wave a hand. "Stand down. Channing, uncuff him."

Channing obeys without a word. I spread my hands. "We come in peace. We just want to talk."

"About what?" Smoke streams from Castor's nostrils, even though his cigarette is long gone.

"About Gabriel Dieter."

Pollux, now free from the silver cuffs, chafes the red marks on his wrists and curses. "We don't fuck with him."

"We just need intel," I say.

"Nah, man," Pollux says, going to stand by his red-haired brother, "We stay out of his way."

Deke speaks up. "You're not strong enough to stand against him, are you?"

Castor sniffs. "He's old, man, real old."

"Dark ages old," adds Pollux.

"You know how old creatures can get," Castor says. His voice twines with his brother's.

"Nothing to live for. Nothing to do but play their mind games."

"Like leeches," I say.

"Right," Castor snaps his finger and another flame dances over his finger tip. "They're bored."

"Bored," I echo.

"Yeah," Pollux turns up the collar of his coat. "They like their games. Dieter's enjoyed putting one over on you."

"The thing is, he's taken someone from us. The best friend of my mate. She was under our protection."

The twins fall silent.

"You don't know me, and I don't know you," I say. "But this woman doesn't deserve to be in Dieter's clutches."

The dragons exchange puzzled looks. "But she's his mate," they say at the same time.

Shit. I was afraid of this.

"He may think that…"

"No, no, man. He was asleep for fucking centuries. He came awake because of her. He's been shaking this world down, searching all over."

"Fuck me," Channing mutters exactly what I'm thinking.

I want to rub my forehead. Fucking dragon smoke giving me a headache. "All we want is to get her back. Make sure she's safe. She doesn't know about our world."

"By now, she does," Pollux mutters.

"All right then," I say. "But it should be her choice."

"You going against the dragon?" Now Castor looks interested. "You better bring reinforcements."

"We can get them."

The twins blink.

"No one goes against Dieter," Pollux says.

Castor still looks intrigued. "We're supposed to warn him if you come. But you know what? I don't think we will."

The twins exchange a grin. One is a mirror image of the other. "If he's bored, let's change up the game."

"You help us, we owe you one," I say.

"Nah, man, you're cool." Castor waves my offer away. He pulls out another cigarette and puts it to his lips before lighting it with his finger tips. "Dieter's been on top too long. Feel free to take him down."

Ten minutes later, Deke, Channing, and I walk out of the alley, leaving the Gemini dragons smoking–literally–in the alley.

I pull out my com. "Colonel, did you get that?"

Colonel Johnson's voice crackles on the other end of the line. "Lance sent me the feed. I heard everything."

"Silver works on dragons. We have confirmation. And now we have Dieter's address. A castle in Romania," Channing reports.

"Good work, boys," Johnson rasps.

"If we're going to do this, we need to bring the whole fucking calvary," I say.

"The cavalry is ready and waiting on your orders," Johnson says.

"Let's do it." I turn to Channing and Deke. "Operation Dragonfall is about to begin."

∽

Gabriel

I sweep around the ballroom floor with Tabitha in my arms. Nothing has ever felt so right. So perfect.

The villagers are as enthralled by her as I am, and she's the perfect hostess even though she doesn't speak Romanian. Her warmth and genuine presence come through her smiles and warm handshakes.

I have to fight my urge not to yank their arms off every time one of them takes her pretty hand in theirs. My dragon can barely withstand the agitation. It's grown steadily worse since we returned to the castle.

He wants me to claim her.

Of course, he does!

I ache for it myself.

But even if Tabitha gave me her consent for the firebrand, I cannot be certain of my dragon. What if I lose control? What if my fire is too hot? What if I combust, or worse–let loose my firepower–when I'm in the throes of desire?

Every night, I make love to her, but it grows harder and harder to hold back. The need is nearly killing me. I have to get up and fly in the middle of the night. In the middle of the day.

I have to jack off in the shower, in my hand, on her belly or thighs, at least four times a day just to keep myself under control.

And tonight it's the worst it's been.

She's in that gorgeous dress, looking like she's ready to be my queen.

Unable to stand it a moment longer, I escort her to where the orchestra is playing and interrupt by taking a microphone. The conductor instantly silences the music.

"My guests," I say in Romanian into the mic. "Thank you all so much for joining us tonight. You are welcome to stay as long as you like, the music and refreshments will go until dawn."

The villagers all cheer, and Tabitha smiles, apparently

understanding it all, despite the language barrier. She waves to Giampi and James, who have been slow dancing in each other's arms all night.

"Come, my beautiful bride. I need to take this dress off of you."

"This does sort of feel like a wedding," she murmurs as she allows me to escort her to the elevator to take her to my tower.

My heart pounds at her words, steam pouring from my nostrils. "Does that mean you're ready to be claimed?" I nearly choke on my words.

She sucks in a breath, blinking. "Um…no."

My heart plummets. Fire stirs in my mercurial center, threatening to erupt. I need to shift and fly, to get control of my dragon before I try to make love to my mate.

"I get forty days and forty nights to decide, Gabriel. Don't push me before it's over."

My skin glows with heat. I pull my hand away from her back in case it's too hot to the touch. "Forgive me, my treasure." Each word comes out with a puff of smoke. The elevator has arrived at the top floor of my tower, but I hit the button to go back down. I need to take her to her chamber before the dragon emerges.

Tabitha turns and looks at me with wide eyes. "What's happening?"

A sense of urgency wraps around my throat like a tight fist. "My dragon is impatient with our arrangement." I hit the elevator button again to return, realizing I don't feel like I can make it in time. I'll have to send her on her own. It's unchivalrous, but I cannot help it.

I step off the elevator but hold up my hand. "Go to your chamber, my love," I say, already stripping off my bow tie and tuxedo jacket.

My stubborn mate refuses, jumping out of the elevator

as the door closes. "No! What's happening? Are you going to shift?"

All I can do is nod as I strip off the tuxedo pants, and my boxer briefs and socks. I work the buttons on my shirt, but I fumble.

Tabitha steps in to help me, her fingers nimble. Her spring rain scent fills my nostrils, making my dragon even more desperate.

"I want to see you," Tabitha says when she frees me of the last button.

I yank off the shirt and pull my undershirt off over my head. "You want to see my dragon?"

"Yes."

"No. It's not safe. Go to your chamber." I run for the open-air turret where I can shift.

"It's safe for me," she insists, chasing me.

Before I can control it, I've changed form. I force my giant head around to keep my dangerous flames from issuing in her direction, but none come out.

There you are. It's Tabitha's voice but in my head.

I flatten myself to the stone floor, spreading my wings low in an offering. Part of me fights it. I should be flying away–keeping a safe distance from my bride–but my dragon-self has other ideas. He wants to keep her close.

I let out a soft, welcoming rumble. A loving chuff. It blows Tabitha's coiffed hair back, but she doesn't look afraid.

Her eyes are bright.

Tabitha runs to my side and strokes her hands over my scales. I can't feel her touch–the scales are far too protective, but the communion, the closeness I have to her is unlike anything I experience when in human form.

Hello, dragon, she murmurs in my mind. Our thoughts

have melded. We are best friends. We are present with one another. We are one.

Tiny streaks of golden lightning flash around my head. My aura—I see what Tabitha sees. Her own aura glows royal purple, tinged with reddish gold.

For a moment, the flash of an image of her riding on my back, her lovely red and gold gown billowing in the breeze, blending in with my dragon scales floats into my mind, and the moment it does, Tabitha gasps.

I would love to ride!

Wait...what is happening? This isn't safe. My dragon's claws click on the flagstones.

But my lovely mate has already determined how to scramble up and finds a seat at my neck, straddling the notch in front of my wings. Her weight is nothing to me, and when she drapes herself along my neck, it feels right.

Let's fly! She speaks into my mind.

My treasure... I try to argue, but my dragon-self overrules me, pushing off from the turret and climbing into the air. My wings beat the air, leaving the stone tower far below.

Tabitha gasps, and I listen closely for a scream or cry of fear, but all I hear is, "Oh!"

Are you all right? It's strange that I can speak with her telepathically.

This is magnificent!

I sense her joy, or perhaps it's coming from my dragon-self—it's hard to tell. All I know is that wave after wave of soul-bursting joy emits through my body and being.

I flap my wings a few times then glide in steady arcs around the area, showing her my land from above. Of course, she can't see in the darkness like I can.

Love.

I'm not sure if it was a spoken word or just a feeling.

I'm not sure whether it came from Tabitha or from me. All I know is that it feels complete. Honest. True.

Love isn't an emotion I considered much before this moment. It wasn't a need for me. I wasn't looking for my mate for love—I was looking for a completion. The final piece of treasure I hadn't been able to amass. The ability to reproduce.

But right now, I'd trade every piece of gold, every land holding, every soldier just to keep feeling this expansion in my chest. This pulsing glow of love that seems like the meaning of life itself.

Love.

This time I know it's me who spoke. My dragon.

I love you, too, beautiful dragon-man. That was Tabitha.

She loves me. Although I would've said it was impossible to feel any more, the sense of love expands even further.

Love. This time flames issue from my mouth—yellow and red billowing into the night. I fly into the cloud of smoke.

Tabitha doesn't shriek. She laughs.

I love you, too, she repeats.

It feels like some kind of miracle. Some impossible feat.

Without thinking, I circle back to the castle and alight more gently and smoothly than I've ever landed. I lower my head, and she slides down my snout to drop to the ground. She's still laughing with delight, like a child on a playground.

I shift and scoop her into my arms, striding swiftly for my bed. The strains of music and laughter of the party-goers carry up to the tower.

Tabitha sucks on my neck. Kisses along my jaw.

I shake with need, unable to rein in my passion. I want to be suave and skilled as her lover, but instead, I'm like a rutting beast. I throw her onto the bed and climb above her, fisting my cock.

Her eyes glaze with the same passion. She lifts the short skirt at the front of her dress and spreads her knees for me. I tear off her panties, shoving into her before they're even down her knees. She kicks them off beneath me, then wraps her legs behind my back, pulling me in, squeezing her tight channel around my pulsing cock.

Love.

It's still my dragon talking.

This is the first time I've heard him in my human form in centuries.

"Tabitha…Tabitha," I chant, plunging in and out of her, synchronizing my thrusts with the lift of her hips, the squeeze of her internal muscles. "My treasure. Tabitha, my treasure."

Firebrand.

My dragon wants me to mark her, to claim her as ours.

"No, we can't," I mutter.

"What?" Tabitha reaches for my face, caressing it in the firelight.

I shake my head. Sweat beads on my chest and forehead. I need to come, but I don't ever want this to stop. I want to please my mate, and I've barely done more than plow into her with a great deal of frenzy and force.

"What is firebrand?" she persists.

"You can hear that?" My treasure's gifts are powerful, indeed. She is connected to the dragon—more than I am.

"What is it?"

My brain is fuzzy. My need coiled so tightly. "It's…how I claim you. When you're ready," I add. I will not claim her before she's agreed. It would be wrong.

Besides, I can't claim her now, I'm way too far out of

my mind. My control is a frayed thread. If I hurt Tabitha…I'd never recover.

"Gabriel." Tabitha's eyelids flicker as her eyes roll back in her head. "It's so good." She arches beneath me.

That's it. My balls draw up tight.

I lose it completely.

I plow into her, forgetting to pull out for the finish. Hot spurts of my cum shoot down my shaft.

Tabitha cries out, her muscles squeezing around my cock, milking it for more.

"Oh God!" I shout, realizing what I'd done. Fire activates in my mercurial center. I yank back, pulling out and spraying the remainder of my essence on the floor as I back up.

"Noooo," Tabitha moans, bringing her fingers between her legs, sinking two of them into her juicy channel as she finishes.

I drop to my knees, dazed with the release and by fear over what I'd almost done.

"Are you all right?" I croak.

Clearly, she is. My cum didn't scald her. She's still healthy and well. Gloriously alive and spectacularly beautiful as she makes herself come with her hand between her legs.

I force myself up on shaky legs and rush to her. "My treasure." I move her hand out of the way to help her finish with my fingers, needing to be the one who makes her come.

She orgasms under my touch, her feet planting firmly on the bed, so she can lift her hips in the air for it.

"My sweet, precious, beautiful mate. I'm sorry. Are you all right? You're not hurt?"

Tabitha pants on the bed, her body falling like a ragdoll into the covers. She blinks her eyes open. "Hurt?"

She sounds dazed. Her caramel locks are in her face, and she shoves them out of the way and props herself up on her elbows. "Hurt by what?"

"Me." I can still barely speak.

Then she reaches for me, and my heart explodes again. She pulls me down on top of her. "Why would I be hurt? Don't be ridiculous, dragon-man." She offers her lips for a kiss.

I dare to give her one. It's tender. Brief.

"That was wonderful," she murmurs against my lips. "I loved it."

I draw in a shaky breath, trying to calm the erratic beating of my heart.

"I love you." It feels important for me to say it. The man, not the dragon.

She smiles against my lips. "I love you, too, Gabriel. You and your dragon."

Something inside me buzzes, but it's with happiness, not the usual agitation. There's an energy—too much pent-up energy—but it's not troubled.

It's … a happy energy.

I roll Tabitha to her side and snuggle into her. We can make this work. We're so close. Any day now, she will accept me, and I'll take great care in giving her my firebrand. I can control the dragon until then.

We're so close.

12

Tabitha

I dream I'm with the dragon in the warm darkness of the treasure-filled cave. I have a ball of light glowing in my hands, and I'm going to give it to the dragon. The light glows reddish-purple, the same color as my heart. Gold lightning flashes around us as I raise my hands to offer up my essence to the dragon.

I will give him my heart, and he will give me his.

But he can't because he's cuffed, his aura suppressed, tucked down inside him. I would reach for it, but I can't get to it.

His wings explode from his back. The blast of air knocks me sideways. He throws back his head. There's a whoosh. He's about to belt fire in this closed space.

"No," I scream but the world turns lava hot. The air boils away. I'm choking. This is the end.

I wake up tangled in silk sheets, gasping. Gabriel is stretched out beside me, still naked. Smoke rises from the bed curtains bundled at each wooden post.

The bed is on fire!

"Gabriel!"

He's awake and on his feet in the same moment. I

reach for him, and he snatches me up. I hug his neck as he carries me out of the tower and down the cold steps.

Shouts and screams echo up from the ballroom and the courtyard. Gabriel races through the twists and turns of the hallways, coming out into a long window-lined hall. Across the courtyard, high above the castle, plumes of flame split the night. The tower is a pillar of fire. Like something out of the bible or bursting from a dragon's mouth.

"Sir." James runs up in an inside-out dressing gown. Giampi's right behind him, his curls standing on end, a blanket around his bare shoulders. The chef offers the blanket to James, who hands it to Gabriel, who swathes us both in it best he can. He lets me stand on my own two feet, but keeps me in the circle of his arms.

James mutters something to Giampi, who nods and runs out of the room, slamming doors in his wake. The rest of us stand in the darkness, shadows and light from the blaze flickering over our faces.

"An emergency helicopter is on its way," James reports. "The security team has initiated the fire safety protocol. They will stop the blaze, thanks to the fire-stopping technology you installed, and the village's increased emergency budget."

Gabriel says nothing. I can hear him blaming himself. I set a hand on his tensed forearm, but his expression doesn't change.

Giampi returns with an armful of blankets and clothing. He and James murmur to each other.

At the end of the room, a black-clad man steps into the doorframe and raps on the gilt trim. "Sir," he addresses Gabriel.

Gabriel starts to pull away, and I cling to him. I don't want to be too needy, but my insides are raw.

Gabriel passes a big hand over my head, his normal grace replaced by clumsiness. "I need to speak with my head of security." He tucks the blanket around me, leaving him naked. "James?"

The butler comes to collect me. Gabriel's handing me off whether I like it or not.

"I will prepare a place in the study for madame to rest," James says.

"Go with Buttons," Gabriel orders me softly. "You will be safe. Please."

"Okay," my voice shakes. There's a blank void around Gabriel's head, contrasting with the soft colors of James and Giampi's auras. My dragon man is still a locked box, and I don't hold the key. "Come to me soon."

⁓

James sets me up in the library and finds me a pair of slippers and a change of clothes. I can't sleep, so I sit and sip the tea he brought me, ignoring the plate of biscotti Giampi sent.

Dawn gilds the window frames before Gabriel finds me. He's in a thick wool sweater and wearing a pair of pants that are tight across his ass and leave several inches of ankle exposed. Less like capris and more like they shrunk in the wash. I've fared better in soft sweatpants and a faded *Forza Azzurri* t-shirt. James must have raided his and Giampi's closets to find clothes for us.

I sit up when Gabriel enters the room. The library is dark and quiet. James was going to turn on the gas fireplace, but I asked him to keep it off. Staring into the flames with the smell of smoke still clinging to my hair didn't seem appropriate.

Gabriel stands in the doorway so long, he could be

asleep on his feet. He's staring at the empty fireplace. I ache to go to him, but something in his expression glues me to the couch.

"How's the fire?" I ask.

"Contained."

"And the tower?"

"Gone."

"Gone?" The insides could turn to ash, but the tower was made of stone.

"The flames were too hot. The mortar gave way."

How did the fire get so hot? I don't ask.

"Dragon fire," Gabriel murmurs. He's still across the room, staring at nothing with ghosts in his eyes. "The dragon got loose for a moment while I slept."

"Gabriel." I hold out my hand to him.

He lurches forward. Instead of sitting down and gathering me into his arms, he falls to his knees on the carpet in front of me and lets his head fall into my lap.

I hunch over him, pressing him close. My fingers dig into his thick black hair.

"My treasure," His voice is muffled. "You could have died." His shoulders are shaking.

"I know. I had a dream that I was dead." I can barely get the words out. "Your dragon–"

"He did this." Gabriel uncoils and pulls away too fast for me to reach. He moves in a blur, rising and pacing across the room fast as a bullet shot from a rifle. His hair is wild. "He killed you."

It seems strange that he says *he* instead of *I*. That there's this separation between his two sides. That's what the gold cuffs in my vision with the dragon are about.

"No." I try to stand, but my legs are too shaky. "I'm okay."

Gabriel jerks his head back and forth. "The first time.

He killed you." Red and gold light dances over his hair. There for a moment and gone the next. Like flames snuffed out by darkness.

"You died," he says, his voice eerily cold. "You were my mate, and you died. You were born hundreds of years ago."

My hand's over my mouth. I don't remember putting it there. I lower it. "I don't remember."

"Thank Fate."

I bite my lip. I believe in past lives, so I'm open to what he's saying. If I lived hundreds of years ago, I would have to die to be reincarnated. It would suck to remember my death.

I prop myself up on the couch arm and head on unsteady legs towards him. He doesn't turn. I put my arms around him and press my face into his back. For a while, we just breathe together.

"Tell me. Tell me everything."

The library is silent but for a ticking grandfather clock in a room three doors over. I jump at a soft *whoosh* and the smell of gas. The library fireplace cut on automatically.

Gabriel's whole body has turned to stone. He's cold. Only the slow rise and fall under his sweater tells me he's alive.

I'm about to say something when he breaks the silence.

"You were a peasant woman. I was hunting in the woods, and I caught your scent. You were a few years younger than you are now, but well past marriageable age. You'd approached spinster age, which had your parents worried." He shakes his head and continues. "When I met you, you were gathering wildflowers. You always skipped out on your chores. You needed freedom."

A sense of certainty steals over me. Gabriel is telling the truth.

"We connected instantly. I wanted to carry you off right there, but I did what was proper. I offered a bride gift to your parents. They were in favor but insisted on a formal wedding.

"Everything was ready when there came word of an uprising. Enemy forces threatening war. I needed to protect you–to make sure our kingdom was safe. For you. I went to defend the borders of my land." His voice is far away. He takes a few steps away, and I let him go, even though I miss his warmth.

"I thought it would be easy. Humans are so fragile. None can stand against the dragon." He rubs a big hand down his face. "I let my dragon free, and we rained fire and death upon everything at the border. Smoke for miles and miles. But there was a windstorm. The fires caught and raged. They spread in an instant."

He turns, and his face is gaunt, shadows smudging the hollows of his cheeks and under his eyes. "I flew to you." He works to swallow. "But it was too late. The fires were so hot. Your village was ash. The church had caught fire and fallen in. The bridal procession…" He squeezes his eyes shut.

This is the final scene in the tapestry.

Humans are so fragile. None can stand against the dragon.

"You were dead. And it was my fault."

I pad closer to him, reaching for his hand. He moves at the last second, blurring and appearing a foot away. "It was my fault."

If he really wants to escape me, he'll have to run farther than that. I close the distance between us and capture his hand, squeezing it to bring him back to me.

"It wasn't your fault," I tell him. "It was an accident. And that's all in the past. Now I'm here. We're together, and we can figure this out. Okay?"

He whirls so quickly, I fall backward. He catches me, his hand closing over the cuff on my wrist.

"No. It's too much." He catches my other wrist and holds my hands between us. "I'm a danger to you. I thought I could keep you safe, but I can't."

"I'm still safe," I cry because I sense something final in his tone. Like he's breaking up with me. I shiver at the coldness in his face.

Gabriel stills. He pulls the sweater he's wearing off and drops it over my head, leaving him in shirtsleeves. His incense-like scent surrounds me, and for a second, I am calm.

Then Gabriel shakes his head. His eyes are dull, his expression blank. "You won't be for long if you remain here. I will have the pilot prep the jet to take you back to New Mexico. I cannot be near you." He turns and strides to the door.

"What? No! Gabriel!" I stumble after him and stop short when he raises a hand.

"You will obey me in this." His voice is frigid. "You will go willingly, or I will deliver you to your friends in a cage."

He waits until I give a stricken nod and exits the room.

I'm left hugging my arms around myself, trying to get warm. I want to run after him, but I can't bear for him to lock me up again. Lock me away, like the dragon.

Just when we were finally getting somewhere, when I'd started to believe this might be possible, he ends it. I can't believe it.

I cover my mouth with my hand and sink into the couch with shaking legs.

I'm going home. Without Gabriel. A few weeks ago, I'd have been happy. Now? My heart is torn apart.

This is wrong. So wrong.

Gabriel

Darkness overcomes me. My rage melds with my dragon-mind, and before I know it, I'm in the sky, shifted from my human form into the great monster who nearly decimated my own castle.

I fly hard and fast, pumping my wings, needing to feel the air against my scales to cool the flames that lick up my throat. I end up over the Black Sea, where I dive into the dark waters, swimming ever deeper, trying to cool the storm inside me.

It doesn't work.

I surface and belch a rage of fire that would've incinerated any ships in a half-mile radius had they been near.

I can't have Tabitha.

I *can't* have her.

Mate, my dragon instinct argues.

You nearly killed our mate! Again!

I belch more fire, boiling the water beneath me. To cool the inferno, I dive beneath the surface again, flapping my wings to propel myself deeper and deeper. Then I come up and take flight again, water streaming off my heated scales, creating clouds of steam.

Gabriel.

Come home.

Oh fate. Fate. She's calling to me. Her voice is inside my head.

And she called my castle home.

A great sob shakes my giant body and I spin in a circle, creating a torrent of wind. A hurricane.

Gabriel.

Come home. I need you here.

Fate!

Before I know it, I've reversed directions. My powerful wings pump in the direction of my castle.

I can't let her call go unanswered. Maybe in my human form I would have more control, but in this shape? Impossible.

The dragon wants Tabitha, and she knows how to speak straight into our mind.

Warning bells go off in my mind a hundred times over as I approach the castle. Warning me that she's in danger?

Or that I'm a danger to her?

I can't decipher it. I'm too foggy-minded, too grief-stricken to realize the danger at the foot of the mountain.

There's a whistling sound and a thud. Fiery pain sizzles through me.

I'm hit.

A puncture-wound right beneath my wing, in the tender place I'm most vulnerable.

I try to keep pumping my wings. I have to get to Tabitha. She may need me. But my wounded wing is useless, barely flapping. I'm plummeting. Fast. My muscles are weak. Unresponsive.

Hit! I somehow convey to her.

Gabriel! Her voice is a scream inside my head.

The ground rises up, and I strike it so hard the earth itself cracks. And then a net flies over me, the burn of silver searing right through my scales.

I lie on my side, chest heaving, unable to move.

Trapped. My dragon sends the word like a telegraph to our mate.

Tabitha
"Gabriel!"

I race blindly through the castle. Something's wrong. Horribly, horribly wrong. I find a heavy door and tug the latch–it swings open. Cold air hits my face, and I rush into the courtyard, skidding on the ice.

A man in black–Gabriel's head of security–jogs up to me. "Ma'am?" he calls.

I rush to him. He side-eyes my slippers and outfit, but I ignore that. "Gabriel's in trouble!" I shriek. "The dragon was hit. He fell from the sky, and now he's trapped."

The man's lips tighten, and he swallows. "I am to allow the wolf pack to enter and collect you," he says stiffly. I can sense the disapproval of his orders in his expression. He nods to the closest side of the courtyard, where the huge doors are creaking open. Wind blasts into the courtyard. My hair whips into my face.

"What?" I jog to the open doors, the head of security at my side. There's a road curving up to the castle, big enough to fit two tanks side by side. But there's no sign of invasion. "Where are they? Are they here?"

"They're approaching now." He holds a pair of binoculars to his eyes and points in the direction of the road far below.

"But where is Gabriel? I think he's hurt."

The man bows his head. "Then he allowed himself to be taken." He glances up at the destroyed tower. Wisps of smoke stream from the charred stone. "He feared it would come to this."

"Come to what?" I rub my forehead. My hair is wild. "Listen to me. Gabriel's been trapped. You have to go rescue him."

"My orders are to stand down and see you safely delivered to the wolf pack."

"I'm not going!" I raise my voice. "This isn't right. None of this is right."

A military convoy rolls into view—three Jeeps equipped with what looks like machine guns and other artillery.

Fuck this. Gabriel's employee isn't going to listen to me.

I half run, half shuffle down the road, heading out of the castle and toward the Jeeps. Gabriel's head of security doesn't follow.

As the calvary comes closer, I wave my arms in the air.

"Tabitha!" Lance, my friend Charlie's boyfriend, leaps from the first Jeep and runs for me.

"Where is the dragon?" I demand, hands on my hips.

Lance's steps stutter, and he slows as he reaches me. "Don't worry, you're safe. We have him contained." His gaze falls to the cuffs around my wrists, then traces my face with signs of concern.

"Why would you do that?" I shout. "Let him go!" I head to the Jeep and climb in the passenger side. "Take me there."

"No way. It's not safe. Dieter is a menace."

"*Now*, Lance!" I shout. "He needs me. I'm his mate!"

"U-uh okay. Hang on a sec." Lance climbs behind the wheel and thankfully starts driving before asking questions. It makes sense—he's a man of action. They all are.

A *wolf*, I remind myself.

He turns the Jeep around and waves his arm in a circle in the air, indicating the following two vehicles should do the same.

"I know what you are," I blurt. "And Gabriel's a dragon, and I think you've hurt him."

He steps on the gas. "He's not hurt. He's contained. But Tabitha, he's very, very dangerous. Intel reports that he incinerated one of the towers last night. Were you in it?"

Tears sting my eyes. "Yes, I was in it. But it was an accident. We were in bed together and he—" My voice hitches.

Lance takes one hand off the wheel to squeeze my

shoulder. "It's okay, sweetheart. We're here now. We'll get you home."

"No," I dash my hand at my face, brushing away tears. "Gabriel is my home. The dragon. I belong to him. I'm his mate. The fire was because...I think his dragon needs to claim me."

Lance whistles. "Fuck. That's a problem. No wonder he's out of control." He gives me a sidelong glance. "Are you going to let him?"

"Yes!" I realize the truth of the word as I shout it. I've been holding back because I could. Because Gabriel gave me forty days and forty nights to make up my mind. But I don't need more time. I've never been more sure of anything in my life. Gabriel Dieter is my mate. Of course I'm going to let him claim me.

"Got it," Lance says, nodding. He catches up to speed quickly. "Then let's get you to the dragon. Maybe it's not too late."

"What do you mean too late?"

Lance keeps his eyes on the road, like he's considering his words. "If a wolf doesn't claim his mate, he can go mad. Moon mad. It means he goes feral. His animal takes over and he can no longer change back to human form. When that happens, he has to be put down."

No.

No, no, no, no, no.

It suddenly all makes sense. This inner struggle Gabriel, the man, has had with Gabriel, the dragon. I can't let anything happen to either of them. I have to save him.

Dust rises behind us on the rocky road as we ride the base of the mountain. I brace myself when Lance takes the Jeep off-road, bumping through a field. A helicopter whirs overhead. In the distance is a plume of smoke and many more military vehicles in a ring around a great form.

"Is that him?" I gasp. "What did you do to him?"

"He's in a silver net to immobilize him. We gave him a tranquilizer, but it's wearing off quickly." Lance's brows snap together. "I don't want you to get too close. He's dangerous in this state, Tabitha."

"Not to me." I say, even though last night's fire did nearly burn me in the bed where I slept. That was an accident. The dragon didn't mean to hurt me. There's a solution to this. Gabriel's given up, but I haven't.

It's up to me.

I close my eyes and try to communicate with Gabriel again. *I'm coming*, I tell him.

The closer we get, the warmer the air. The dragon's fire turned the winter day balmy. The helicopter has landed close by, its blades continuing to swing in lazy rotation.

A blast of fire shoots into the sky, and artillery fire booms.

"Tabitha, you might just make this worse," Lance says as he pulls up at the outer ring of vehicles. "If Gabriel thinks we're keeping you from him, his dragon may go wild. If this is the version of moon madness for dragons, he's out of control."

I ignore Lance's warning and scramble out of the Jeep. The snow has melted in this part of the field. My slippers slap over mushy grass as I weave through the parked vehicles, heading for the trapped dragon. The brilliant red and gold form is hunched on its side, trapped by the tight silver net. My chest gets tight.

"Gabriel," I cry, running for him.

Deke steps out from behind a green tank and catches me in his arms. "Tabitha, calm down. We–"

The dragon's head jerks up, and then he bellows as if in pain.

"That net is hurting him!" I scream, fighting Deke. "Take it off!"

But Lance was right. The sight of me makes the dragon go wild. I don't hear any words in my head, but I can feel the fierce protectiveness. My agitation enrages the dragon further.

He roars and bursts out of the silver net.

His wings unfurl, fire flares out. The blast of heat roasts my face like I've stuck it in an oven. Smoke billows where the dead grasses of winter have caught fire under the melted snow.

Soldiers shout, scrambling.

"Fuck," Deke mutters.

I twist and break free as the dragon's wedge head rears up, it's maw opening wide.

"No!" I scream. Deke slams into me, pushing me behind a tank as a fireball detonates close by. Grasses crackle and the air shimmers.

The fleeing soldiers are dark shapes against the yellow flame. Across the way, Rafe grabs a silver-haired man in a US Army uniform, and they both leap behind a row of metal barrels. Another flash of fire and the equipment explodes.

This is bad. Gabriel might have just incinerated all my friend's mates. The dragon is out of control.

Gabriel's giant wings unfurl, and he launches into the sky. The backwind blasts us, fanning the flames on the ground. The dragon's form dips slightly, as one wing seems to be injured. It fights to flap higher.

I need to calm down. I grab Deke's arm. "Get me to that helicopter."

Deke hesitates.

"Now," I scream.

"He just needs to claim his mate," Lance shouts to Deke from behind me. "Tabitha may be the answer."

Deke nods and scoops me up, dashing across the empty field.

A huge guy in aviator shades sits in the pilot seat, his tattooed biceps stretching the sleeves of his army green t-shirt.

"Got a passenger for you, Teddy," Deke hollers. I scramble from his arms into the passenger seat.

"How high can you fly?" I ask the pilot.

"High as you want, baby girl." Teddy flips a bunch of switches and then pauses to flip up his shades. His eyes flare with an orange light. "Holy shit. You're the dragon's old lady."

"Mate," I nod. "I'm his mate." I point up to the sky, where the dragon is circling. Any moment it could wheel around and blast fire at us again. "I need to be up there–with him."

"Ten-four, dragon mama. Let's get this warbird in the air."

I dig my nails into the sides of the seat. The helicopter engine whines and the blades whir louder and louder.

"You got a plan?" Teddy shouts, throttling the controls. The blades overhead clack and the ground pulls away.

"Sorta," I holler back. Down below, Deke stands shading his eyes, his hair blowing in the wind.

Teddy dips his chin. He's flying with a strange lady to chase down a dragon, and he's not ruffled at all.

A gust blows the helicopter sideways. I grip the seat. "Hang on," he warns. "You don't got a parachute like I do."

I brace myself as we gain height. "I don't need one."

The dragon wheels in the air, turning and flying low

over the military group. Rafe and the silver-haired man have emerged from their blackened hiding place, arms outstretched with guns in hand. The air pops over and over.

"No," I hunch, gasping. They're shooting at the dragon.

Teddy holds a com. He's shouting, "Hold your fire! Repeat, hold your fire!"

The dragon swoops and grabs a tank, tipping it over. Soldiers take cover, shouting.

I close my eyes and find my center. This is my gift, and I've always had it. In my mind, my psychic powers unfurl like dragon's wings.

It's okay, I tell the angry red pulse of light that's the dragon. *I'm here. I'm with you. I'm yours.*

The dragon roars.

"Shit," Teddy barks. My eyes fly open as the helicopter tips.

"It's okay," I bawl. "Fly higher. We need to be higher!"

The helicopter floats upward. Below us is a blanket of black smoke. The dragon's wedged head slices through the heart of the huge cloud. Its long neck spears the billowing black, its wings and whipping tail chasing the rolling smoke away. It's given up belching fire at the soldiers to chase us.

I reach out a hand as if I could touch him. *I'm here.*

We're high enough. The military-occupied field is a smoking gray spot far below. I rise from my seat, gripping the console as the wind whips around me.

"What the fuck are you doing?" Teddy shouts.

My heart somersaults, threatening to break out of my chest. This is crazy. "It's the only way," I scream and inch forward. I'm at the edge of the helicopter, leaning into empty air.

This is going to be one hell of a trust fall. *Dragon, I need you to catch me.*

I launch myself into the freezing air. My arms fly up, my hair whipping back.

For a moment, there's silence. My chest hurts like my insides are shutting down. The ground is fast approaching.

A primordial roar fills my ears, and a great shadow closes over my body. I slam against the cage of its claws.

He caught me. Frozen tears coat my cheeks. *I'm safe.*

My mouth is open, but I don't scream. I'm terrified. I don't want to further agitate the dragon. I curl into a ball in the bony claw, blindly rubbing at the dragon's scales.

We're safe, I tell him. *Both of us. We're together. And safe.*

Wind whips over my face. I squint between the dragon's claws.

The silver-grey outline of the castle appears, the blackened tower swaddled in mist. The dragon snaps his wings, his entire body streamlined into a red-gold arrow angling downwards, aiming straight for the mountain. We're going to crash into the side of the cliff. But when we get closer, a dark slit in the mountainside grows larger, becoming a cave mouth that's large enough to fit a dragon.

I squeeze my eyes shut. The only sound is the whistling wind and the creaking of the dragon's wings.

When I open my eyes again, everything is dark. The air is cool and smoky. There's an incense scent that's familiar.

We're in the dragon's cave.

He sets me down, and metal clinks beneath my feet. I remember the treasure from my vision.

This is his lair. It's real.

I catch my breath and wait until the dragon's settled. "A little light?" I say.

Torches flare to life all around the giant cavern. The space is bigger than the castle courtyard.

"Gabriel." I run toward the dragon, who settled far away from me, as if still afraid of hurting me. In the flicker of torchlight, I can see his scales have been burned in a criss-cross pattern—the silver net injured him.

I want to weep, but I keep it together. I must keep it together.

"Gabriel, it's all right." I run to him, and he lowers his great head. I throw my arms wide and wrap them around his giant snout in an attempted embrace. "I love you. I'm ready for you to claim me. I won't leave you. Okay? I need you to come back to me. I need Gabriel, the man now, please."

The dragon snorts with anger, and I'm lifted off the ground when he shakes his head. I let go and drop to my feet. "Whoa. Easy, boy. I need the man back. Can you shift back for me?"

The dragon shakes his glorious head like he's angry with Gabriel the man. I look around the cave. It's just like it was in my dream where the dragon was in gold cuffs like the pair I wear. Like the dragon is relegated to this cave, hidden, no!--*locked*-away-by Gabriel, the man.

Perhaps now he's locked the man part up, refusing to set him free. The two sides of Gabriel have been at war for hundreds of years over…

Me.

Over the dragon killing me in his past life.

So when he accidentally set fire to the bed last night, Gabriel decided I wasn't safe and tried to keep his dragon self away from me, which only made the dragon more unstable.

You can't keep any part of you locked away without eventually facing the consequences. Perhaps the fire was *a result* of Gabriel's efforts to keep the dragon in chains rather than a reason he should continue with such foolish actions.

"Give him back," I say gently, reaching out to stroke his snout. "I won't let him cuff you or control you anymore."

The dragon lowers his snout to the ground.

"You would never hurt me, would you?"

The dragon shakes its mighty head.

"What happened last night?"

Need you, the dragon says. *Firebrand.*

"You need to claim me?"

A puff of smoke comes from the dragon, and I take it as a yes.

"Gabriel was holding you back because I wasn't ready," I explain. "But I am now. You can have me. Both sides of you can have me. I'm yours."

The dragon shudders, and then the giant form disappears, replaced by Gabriel's beautiful bronze-skinned form, naked and glorious. Gabriel's skin is charred with a miniature version of the criss-cross pattern like it shrunk with him when he changed size. Around him glows an aura—the one that had been missing since the day I met him. It shimmers in shades of pink and green—love and vitality.

"Gabriel!" I run to him and wrap my arms around him, helping him to his feet. "Are you all right? You're burned! Why did you let them hurt you like that?"

He lets out a shaky exhale but doesn't speak. He takes my face in both his hands and stamps his lips over mine.

It's a claiming kiss—the kind I've been waiting for since we first made love. Full of passion and determination. He slides his tongue between my lips, stroking mine open, deepening the kiss. Every change of angle, every breath takes us deeper into it until my limbs are loose, and my body's forgotten all the recent trauma.

The cuffs fall from my wrists.

13

Gabriel

My thoughts were a storm of lightning and flame. And then she appeared. Tabitha, my light in the darkness. My fire in the night. My mate. She sighs and shudders against me, and I hitch her closer. The ancient coins slide under my feet. I could take her right here, right now—

"Sir?" Hess calls from the mouth of the cave.

I ease back from Tabitha's sweet lips. "Yes." I don't take my gaze from hers. There's love swirling in her eyes, and it nearly drops me to my knees.

"The wolf pack is here, sir. To assure Miss Tabitha's safety."

My mouth works. It's hard to find the words, but I do. "We're coming out now."

"Leaving some clothes for you here at the mouth of the cave, sir."

I lean on Tabitha as we make our way over piles of coins and gemstones. She finds the clothes and helps me dress. The soft shirt and pants chafe my burned skin, but by the time I'm clothed, I'm feeling more steady and able to escort Tabitha out from the cave.

A motley crew of soldiers has found a way to reach the mouth of my dragon's cave. In addition to Rafe, Deke, Lance, and Channing, members of the Black Wolf pack, there's Theodore Whitaker, their former helicopter pilot. Colonel Johnson himself stands with his former soldiers. The entire group is covered in soot, like most everything on my property today.

Tabitha wraps both her arms around my waist, hugging me sideways as we walk as if to show her friends she's with me. I drape my arm across her shoulders.

My shoulders ache. My skin burns from the silver, and my gut churns from the tranq they hit me with, not to mention the angst of the past twelve hours, but I force my face into its usual smooth expression.

"Gentleman. Welcome to my home." I extend an arm in the direction of the castle as if I am a gracious host, and they have arrived at my invitation to dance at a ball.

Hess stands behind me, his hand on his weapon, his expression forbidding. His men will have secured the area, and Colonel Johnson's former team members know it. The group of them stand like soldiers–their gazes alert, taking in everything around us, scanning the surroundings, and assessing danger.

Rafe ignores me. "Tabitha, are you okay?"

"I'm fine, but Gabriel's not," she says hotly. "He's burned all over from that net you trapped him in."

"Rafe acted to protect you. We cannot fault his team for that," I say.

Rafe's gaze flicks to me now. He seems slightly surprised at my graciousness.

"We thought you were a prisoner here. You hadn't responded to any messages, and your GPS has been disabled. Adele said the email you sent didn't sound like you," Rafe explains.

"Told you the email wouldn't work," Tabitha mutters to me, even as she presses her body even closer to mine. "Gabriel and I are working on that. His dragon is... protective and more than a little possessive. A trait I've noticed you all exhibit as well."

"Plus he's going moon mad, or whatever the dragon version of that is," Rafe's brother, Lance, explains.

Moon mad. Perhaps some of that in addition to the long-term stand-off I've been in with my dragon over losing Tabitha in her last lifetime.

I drop a kiss on the top of her head. Her acceptance of me, her defense on my behalf is a balm to my bruised state of mind. I just obliterated an entire tower of the castle because of my lust for her, yet still, she stands by my side. Even more miraculously, she affirmed she's my mate. She's willing and ready to be claimed.

There is still danger of me harming her, but my dragon feels calm. At peace. I don't sense the rage or disquiet anymore. Even the lust has softened into a more stable form of love.

The fact that Tabitha can communicate with my dragon side is another miracle. All this time, I was trying to control him, but I don't need to. She commands him as our mate. He will always heed her wishes, hear her cries if she's in danger, and protect her. My dragon will keep her safe.

"My courtship methods may have been a bit... medieval," I concede. "But we have come to an accord." I level a steady look at Rafe. "Tabitha is my mate. She is willing to be fully claimed and receive my firebrand."

"Whoa, man. TMI." The younger operative, Channing, holds up a hand and looks away, shaking his head in mock disgust. "We don't need the deets about how a dragon claims his mate." He shudders.

Tabitha laughs softly.

"Is that true, Tabitha?" Rafe asks my mate. "You're willing to be claimed?"

"Yes." The fact that she doesn't hesitate even for a second heals me even more.

"There are a number of your business dealings the United States government would like to understand," Colonel Johnson said.

"I'm sure there are," I say smoothly. "I would be happy to meet with you at a later time, but at the moment, I am rather preoccupied with my new mate."

"Understandable," Colonel Johnson grunts. "I expect you to take a call from me next month, though."

"As a courtesy, I will take the call, but I will remind you that I do not answer to you or your government."

"Okay, okay. No pissing contest necessary," Rafe says. "Tabitha, you're sure you're okay?" He studies her as if looking for some secret signal from her.

"I'm fine. Gabriel will return my phone to me today, and I'll call everyone back in Taos to reassure them." She looks up at me with brows raised.

"Of course, my treasure."

"All right, then." Rafe steps forward. There's wariness in his pose, but he offers a hand for me to shake.

I accept the offer and clasp his hand.

"Take good care of her," Rafe can't resist warning me. The unspoken part of the sentence is *or else we'll be back.*

I curl my lips to show my fangs. A smile and a threat. "She is royalty here."

"It's true," Tabitha says.

Enough of this dominance posturing. I step back and

sweep Tabitha up into my arms. "If you'll forgive me, I have a bride to claim."

"That's what's up," the pilot, Theodore, gives me a thumbs up, even as Channing mutters, "Fucking gross. Keep it to yourself, dragon. We don't need to hear that shit."

"Thanks for the attempted rescue, guys!" Tabitha calls over my shoulder. "It was unnecessary, but I appreciate the gesture."

"Yep. Anytime," Rafe rumbles.

I hear the slam of doors on the Jeeps and then the vehicles departing, but my attention is focused solely on my beautiful treasure. My sweet bride.

"I can't wait to make you mine," I murmur.

Tabitha twines her arms around my neck and nips my ear. "I already am yours, dragon. I think I always was."

~

Tabitha

By the time Gabriel kicks open the door to my bedroom, I'm cracking up. "I want to be in the room when Rafe tells Adele about today," I say.

"That can be arranged." He doesn't let me down but carries me straight to the bed. "But first, it is time for me to claim you, my treasure."

I'm woozy with the aftermath of adrenaline. I'm barefoot—the slippers I was wearing are long gone. My cheeks are flushed, my hair is wild. The insane magnetism between us crackles like electricity, and arousal pulses between my legs.

I cup his cheek, molding my fingers over his jaw, his brows, his beard. "I'm glad things worked out. There was a moment with the dragon, I wasn't sure he was going to allow you to come back to me."

"He spoke to me."

"He did?"

"Yes. We are now one. Because of you." Gabriel turns his head and kisses my palm.

"And now you're going to claim me," I whisper. I crane my head to meet his lips and gasp as a fireball of heated need rolls through me. I wriggle, stripping off the sweater he gave me and the rest of my clothes. I want nothing between us.

Gabriel takes my clothes and tosses them in the corner, pausing to drink me in.

"What are you thinking?" I reach to help him with his shirt.

"The fire branding may hurt you," he says.

"I like a little pain." I bounce my brows.

He remains solemn, slowly shucking off his clothes.

"Are you nervous?" I ask.

"I don't want to hurt you."

Sweet dragon man. "Trust yourself," I say. "And trust me."

Naked now, he steps close to the bed. I examine his hardened chest. Hovering a finger in the air, I trace the lines where the net marked him.

"Does it hurt?" I ask.

"Not anymore."

I bend my head and press a butterfly light kiss to the burned skin.

"My sweet mate," Gabriel rumbles.

He leans forward, but I push him back, guiding him to lie down. I curl a fist around his proud cock. He stretches out, six feet plus of bronzed beauty. This is the first time he's let me be on top, in control.

"Suck me," he orders, and I grin. He's still in control.

Licking my lips, I lower my head. He tastes like smoke and spice. I curl my tongue around him and hum, working my neck up and down. He fills my mouth so perfectly. My pussy aches, ripe and juicy.

"Tabitha," he calls, but I continue to bob my head, sucking so hard I hollow my cheeks. "Tabitha." He tugs my head up by my hair, growling, "It's time."

He has to help me straddle him. He's still gripping my hair, maneuvering me into position. I spread my thighs wide, guiding his hard rod to my slippery sex. He snaps his hips, driving into me with full force, filling me. My head flies back. Only his grip on me keeps me upright.

"Ride me, my treasure." With his free hand, he covers my left breast, squeezes, smacks it. The slap transmutes to a spear of pure pleasure, slicing through my core and spurring me to motion. My inner muscles ripple, clenching impossibly tight until Gabriel is part of my body. There is no separation between us. We are interlocking circles, woman and man and beast becoming one.

"Give yourself to me," Gabriel grunts. "Now."

Heat blossoms in my belly and rolls through me. The sensation spreads up my back, like someone ran a warm glove up my spine. I rock over Gabriel, my body undulating out of my control.

Red and gold flames flicker on the edges of the bed. They're not real—they blend with the pink and green and purple of our auras. Every cell in my body tightens. An explosion is brewing inside me, fire and heat and power caught in the crucible, ready to blow.

"Yes!" Gabriel shouts.

A flash of light—a red and gold supernova—blinds me. I cry out. The heated cape on my shoulders slices into my skin. It doesn't hurt—it feels like a metamorphosis. Awakening. Becoming.

Wings of fire blast from my back. Gabriel is under me, grounding my body when I'd float off the bed.

The light disappears, and I'm left blinking. Red sunspots dance in front of my eyes.

"It is done," Gabriel growls.

The flames around the bed are gone. So are the wings I saw with my psychic gifts.

There's a fading heat on my back. I twist, but I can't see, and I don't dare touch. If that was a vision, why is my skin so warm?

Gabriel sits up, steadying me. Keeping me in his lap, he swings us off the bed and lifts me with his palms under my ass. He carries me to the gilt-framed mirror in the corner of the room.

Something glimmers on my back. I blink, but it's not an illusion. At the base of my spine, three interlocking circles shimmer red. *Borromean rings.* When the light hits them, they shine gold.

I'm marked with a mystical tattoo. My flesh will forever bear the same symbol as the dragon's scales.

"The firebrand," Gabriel murmurs. His aura is a soft sunset around his head.

"I'm yours," I breathe.

"Yes." He bows his head, resting his forehead against mine. We're pressed together, heart to heart, our bodies joined and our spirits entwined. "We are one."

"I think we should have a wedding," I say, only because his castle is the perfect place for a destination wedding. "Invite my mom and all my friends from Taos. And the villagers. Like the Christmas ball."

"No," Gabriel says. "It will be far grander than the Christmas ball. I will spare no expense for my bride."

I smile. "You know I'd be just as happy with a barefoot backyard wedding, right?"

He looks confused. "Is that what you want?"

"No, I'm a dragon's bride. I should have a grand castle wedding."

He kisses my nose. "The grandest of all weddings."

"I love you, dragon-man," I murmur.

"I never knew love before you," he confesses. "I am a changed man."

EPILOGUE

THREE MONTHS LATER

Tabitha

The snow has mostly melted in Taos ski valley by late March. There are a few white patches in the shadows of the pine trees, on the edge of the Black Wolf pack's lawn.

Gabriel opens my door and offers me his hand. I swing out of the Aston Martin, not bothering with my coat.

"Are you warm enough, my treasure?" Gabriel asks, examining my bare arms.

"All good." I've always had a high cold tolerance, but since the firebrand, I might as well be impervious to the winter chill. Which is good because all of Gabriel's houses seem to be in remote, snowy places. You'd think the dragon would prefer the heat, but no.

I tuck my hair behind my ear. It's been a month since I've seen my friends and their mates, and I'm strangely nervous.

"You look lovely," Gabriel assures me, offering his arm.

"You know, you don't have to wear a suit to dinner. It's probably going to be a cookout."

"I will eat with the wolves. I will not dress like them."

I roll my eyes. *Stuffy old dragon.*

"I heard that," he growls in a tone that promises delicious retribution.

I take his arm and let him lead me up the driveway. He places a hand over mine.

"If at any point you want to leave, speak into my mind, and I will ensure you get your wish."

I love how open I can be about my psychic gifts. My abilities are growing stronger, thanks to practice with my mate. "And if I want to say *I love you*, I'll tug my ear."

Gabriel looks at me blankly, even though I know he gets the reference.

"Thank you," I say. "But these are my friends, Gabriel. It'll be fine."

He nods, but I hear his unspoken grunt. *It better be.*

I hide my smile. He takes his protection duties very seriously.

As we walk up to the front door of the lodge, Gabriel's fingers find the thick gold band I wear on my ring finger. I wasn't a huge fan of wedding rings or weddings, but my mother insisted. She also hired lawyers to review our prenup and was mollified when it merely stated that all Gabriel's wealth belonged to me.

We had a big ole wedding at the castle, as traditional as it could be. My friends were bridesmaids, and the whole village was invited. Giampi made six wedding cakes.

The wedding rings we wear are made of the same material Gabriel designed for the cuffs. Two small cuffs—one for him, one for me.

I still wear the cuffs, of course. During sexy times.

The front door to the lodge opens before I can ring the doorbell. Rafe stands there, and for a tense few seconds, he and Gabriel stare at each other.

"Dragon," Rafe jerks his chin up.

"Wolf," Gabriel replies. I squeeze his arm.

"Human," I put in my own imitation of a manly growl. "Mate."

Both Rafe and Gabriel look at me.

"Meat," I grunt. "Booze. Now."

Rafe's cheek twitches, and he steps back. "Come on in."

The Black Wolf pack's lodge smells like heaven's kitchen. Adele must be cooking.

"Lucy, I'm home!" I shout halfway down the hall.

Gabriel dips his head close. "*I Love Lucy*, 1950s sitcom."

"That's right," I whisper back. We round the corner to enter the living room.

"Tabitha!" Charlie and Sadie cry. My friends are lounging with their respective boyfriends. Their mates.

There's a rush of hugging. We're joined by Adele, who clomps from the kitchen in her apron and high heels.

"You'd think you'd haven't seen me for a year. Not a month," I pretend to grumble from the center of the hug-huddle.

"There wasn't a ton of socializing after the wedding. Not when Mr. Dragon wanted to fly you off to Paris for a honeymoon," Sadie teases.

"It was Italy and Paris and Switzerland, remember?" Charlie says.

"Right," I say. "Gabriel does nothing in half measures."

All our mates are on their feet, standing in a loose circle around us. Lance in particular looks watchful, wary. As soon as the hugging ends, he tugs Charlie into his arms and folds them both into a huge armchair. His hands cover her burgeoning belly.

Deke is a tall, dark shadow by the fireplace. He wears a

forbidding expression. But that's Deke. He has resting badass face.

Gabriel has his hands in his pockets, but a smoky, spicy scent like charred cinnamon fills the room.

I go to him and thread an arm in his. "You all know Gabriel."

"Oh yes. I'll never forget a man who flew me and all your bridesmaids to Paris for dress fittings." Adele gives Gabriel a smile, which reduces the level of tension in the room.

From what I gather, wolf shifters and dragon shifters don't mix. They're used to seeing each other as a threat and really don't like each other in their homes or around their mates.

On top of that, Gabriel and the Black Wolf pack don't have the best history. Something about Rafe and the ops team breaking into his chalet, and Gabriel thinking Adele was his mate because she was wearing the scarf I gave her.

I've had long conversations with Gabriel about how to repair the relationship after he played all his little games.

Seeking Adele's forgiveness was paramount. The trip to Paris and unlimited shopping spree helped a lot. Plus Gabriel was the perfect host during our wedding.

"Yeah, still not sure if I'm over you fucking with my mate," Rafe growls.

"I returned her to you when I realized my error," Gabriel counters. "And I destroyed her enemies in the meantime."

"Yeah, about that," Lance interjects. "You can't just go incinerating drug cartels in their homes with dragonfire. It confuses the hell out of the local authorities."

I stare at Gabriel. "You did that?"

"They were after Adele," he says as if that explains everything. "And I thought she was you."

"Don't tell me you wouldn't have done the same," Gabriel says to Rafe.

"We try to follow human laws," Rafe says stiffly.

"Bullshit," Deke coughs into his fist.

"Well, we cover our tracks better when we do clean house," Lance explains. "You need to up your game there, dragon."

"Perhaps you're right," Gabriel says. I love him for being conciliatory.

"Excuse me, I need to check the roast," Adele says. "Rafe can get you a glass of wine."

"Need help?" I ask.

"No." She flaps her hand at us as she heads back to the kitchen. "You guys relax."

Rafe follows her to fetch the wine. Lance and Charlie are already curled up in the armchair. Deke sits on the stone fireplace ledge and pulls Sadie onto his lap.

Gabriel and I settle on a loveseat together. He looks so formal with his suit and straight posture, I surreptitiously stick my fingers in his hair and mess it up.

"You're too pretty," I murmur.

"How long will you guys be in Taos?" Charlie asks.

I twist to her. "I was thinking we'd stay for a while. There's Sadie's wedding, and of course, I want to meet the baby."

"Oh, that's lovely," Sadie pipes up.

"We have a place near Angel Fire," I say.

"Not staying in the train car?" Charlie teases.

"No, I turned that into my studio," I say. "Gabriel got us a chalet. You guys can come visit. It's nice." The chalet is a twenty-bedroom mansion on a private mountain, with its own helipad. *Nice* can't begin to describe it.

"Sounds great." Sadie drinks us all in. "Look at us. Just

a few months ago, none of us were dating. Now we all have mates."

"Where's Channing?" I ask.

"On a road trip," Lance says. "He's been doing that more lately–going off on his own."

"Maybe he's going to see a woman." Charlie bounces her brows.

"Or two. Or five. Player's gonna play," Lance says. Charlie rolls her eyes and Lance nuzzles her neck. The expression on his face is so tender, I look away to give them privacy.

"Dinner!" Adele calls, and we tromp to the dining room and let Adele arrange us in the seats the way she wants. There are huge covered dishes lining the center of the table.

"I hope it's all right. I set it up family-style," Adele says, pointing out the green bean casserole, mashed potatoes, salad, and roast beef.

"It's perfect." I grin at Gabriel. "That means you're family."

"Family," he echoes.

"Yep." Charlie sinks into her chair and pats her stomach. "Hope you're up for babysitting."

"Hell, no," Lance mutters. "I am not letting my pup go near a dragon."

"I don't eat pups," Gabriel says mildly.

"Maybe you'll be the ones babysitting," I say lightly.

Adele gasps.

"Oh, do you have news?" Sadie asks. Beside her, Deke fills his plate with a leaning tower of beef.

"Not yet." I flush. Gabriel and I had a long discussion about modern birth control. Turns out he knew from the start that I'd had an implant. At any point, he could've ordered it removed. I asked him to give me a year or two to get used to the idea, and then he has free rein to 'breed' me.

I can hardly wait.

The rest of the meal goes smoothly, mostly because the wolves are too busy stuffing their faces, leaving me and my friends to carry the conversation.

After dessert, Charlie says, "One day, when I can travel again, I'd love to come back to Romania. Do more sightseeing."

"You're welcome anytime," I say.

"I hear there's a real dragon who lives there," she teases. "You know, when I was a child, I was obsessed with dragons. I'm so happy to know they really exist."

"There are very few of us left in this world," Gabriel says solemnly. "But hopefully we can add a few more." He kisses the top of my head.

Charlie claps her hands. "Baby dragons would be the best."

Gabriel angles his head towards her. "Do you want to see my dragon?"

Charlie gasps. "Really? You would do that? That'd be epic."

"I have procured a suitable flight pad nearby."

"The fuck?" Deke mutters.

As one, the wolves and Gabriel rise from the table. Sadie and Adele and I leap to our feet. The tension ratchets up in the room.

"What are you talking about, honey?" I trill, taking Gabriel's arm.

"Follow me." The tips of Gabriel's canines flash with his enigmatic smile.

"Still playing games," Rafe murmurs, but the pack follows Gabriel and me out of the house and to the edge of the lawn. When we head into the forest, I'm dancing with curiosity.

A faint trail through the leaves leads us to a large patch of cleared land. We traipse out of the woods and fan out in the vast bare lot.

"Seriously, dragon?" Lance says. "You bought this place?" He turns in a circle and kicks a big clump of dirt out of his way. "I thought they were going to build a big house here."

"I figured this would be convenient for our purposes." Gabriel has shed his suit jacket. He bends to remove his socks and shoes. "Seeing as we are 'family' now."

Rafe looks profoundly unhappy.

Deke turns to his alpha. "We really gonna let him come and go as he pleases?" he grunts one of the longest sentences I've heard from him.

"Yes," Rafe grits out. "We have a truce. Right, Dieter?"

"That is correct." Gabriel unbuttons his dress shirt and tosses it on a nearby branch. The sunlight strokes lovingly down the breadth of his lean muscles.

"Besides," Rafe says. "those in the know will assume we're allies with a dragon. His presence makes us safer."

"Because he's a protective bastard." Lance's statement is barely audible, which might as well be a shout for those with shifter hearing.

"He's my protective bastard," I amend.

Adele claps her hands, and we all jump. "That's settled then," she says. "You can visit anytime, both of you. Just text ahead, so I can put a pot of coffee on."

"We will," I promise. "We won't show up without advance notice unless it's unavoidable. Right, Gabriel?"

"Of course, my treasure," he answers smoothly.

My friends and my smiles balance out the wolves'

glares. To Rafe's credit, he says nothing about installing anti-aircraft weaponry around his lodge.

"My bride?" Gabriel extends his hand. "Shall we fly home?"

"What about your car?" Adele asks.

"I can send someone to fetch it," Gabriel says.

"Fuck that," Lance says. "You leave your car, I'm going joyriding."

Gabriel tilts his head. "The key fob is in my jacket pocket. You are welcome to enjoy a ride."

Lance whoops. Deke mutters something about a "flex".

I let Gabriel lead me further into the empty clearing. He kisses my hand and steps away, striding towards the woods opposite. Between one step and another, a dragon explodes from his form. Its red and gold scales shine like rubies and gold coins in the sunlight.

"Holy shit," Sadie gasps. We all look at her. Sadie's a kindergarten teacher, and she never swears.

"What?" she squeaks. "He's huge."

Deke pulls her against him. Lance is holding Charlie and Rafe looks ready to scoop Adele up and run for cover.

"It's all right, guys," I say. "He's tame." I stroll closer and reach up to stroke the dragon's scaled jaw.

My cheeks stretch wide with a grin as I head around Gabriel's huge body. He offers a claw to help me swing up and settle on his shoulders. I flatten my body to his scaly neck, my skin soaking in the heat and spice of him.

His wings pump, and we're aloft. As we clear the trees, the dragon scales shimmer and reflect the blue of the sky.

The wind tugs at my hair. Below us, dust billows around the clearing, and my friends retreat to the treeline where they watch, shading their eyes.

The invisible wings pump around me, and Gabriel wheels away from the brown patch of earth that's the cleared flight pad. Our shadow races below us, sweeping over the pines. We're flying higher and higher. Behind us, the lodge is a tiny Tinker toy. Thrills run up my spine. We swoop over the summit, gliding over the rocky face.

The world falls away. There's nothing but the high mesa before me, an endless blue sky around me, the dragon under me, and my laughter rippling over the wind.

∽

Thank you so much for reading Alpha's Fire! If you enjoyed it, we would so appreciate your review. They make a huge difference for indie authors.

Be sure you've signed up for our newsletters to get word of the next books in the series—featuring Teddy, Channing, and a bunch of grumpy bears we haven't even introduced yet!

Join Renee's Romper Room and Lee Savino's Goddess Group on Facebook to chat about the books and become a part of the Bad Boy Alpha community. Huge hugs—we adore you!

WANT MORE?

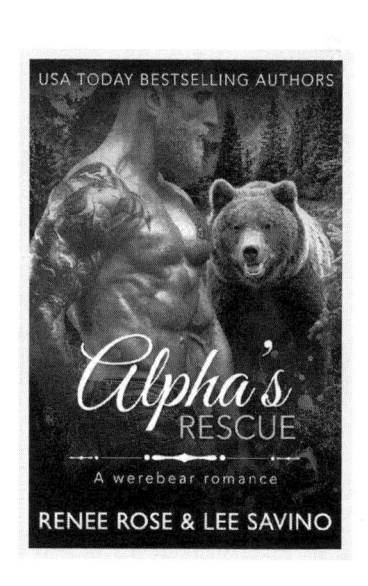

WANT FREE BOOKS?

Go to http://subscribepage.com/alphastemp to sign up for Renee Rose's newsletter and receive a free books. In addition to the free stories, you will also get special pricing, exclusive previews and news of new releases.

Download a free Lee Savino book from www.leesavino.com

OTHER TITLES BY RENEE ROSE

Chicago Bratva

"Prelude" in Black Light: Roulette War

The Director

The Fixer

"Owned" in Black Light: Roulette Rematch

The Enforcer

The Soldier

The Hacker

The Bookie

The Cleaner

Vegas Underground Mafia Romance

King of Diamonds

Mafia Daddy

Jack of Spades

Ace of Hearts

Joker's Wild

His Queen of Clubs

Dead Man's Hand

Wild Card

Contemporary
Daddy Rules Series

Fire Daddy

Hollywood Daddy
Stepbrother Daddy

Master Me Series

Her Royal Master
Her Russian Master
Her Marine Master
Yes, Doctor

Double Doms Series

Theirs to Punish
Theirs to Protect

Holiday Feel-Good

Scoring with Santa
Saved

Other Contemporary

Black Light: Valentine Roulette
Black Light: Roulette Redux
Black Light: Celebrity Roulette
Black Light: Roulette War
Black Light: Roulette Rematch
Punishing Portia (written as Darling Adams)
The Professor's Girl
Safe in his Arms

Paranormal

Two Marks Series

Untamed

Tempted

Desired

Enticed

Wolf Ranch Series

Rough

Wild

Feral

Savage

Fierce

Ruthless

Wolf Ridge High Series

Alpha Bully

Alpha Knight

Bad Boy Alphas Series

Alpha's Temptation

Alpha's Danger

Alpha's Prize

Alpha's Challenge

Alpha's Obsession

Alpha's Desire

Alpha's War

Alpha's Mission

Alpha's Bane

Alpha's Secret

Alpha's Prey

Alpha's Sun

Shifter Ops

Alpha's Moon

Alpha's Vow

Alpha's Revenge

Alpha's Fire

Midnight Doms

Alpha's Blood

His Captive Mortal

All Souls Night

Alpha Doms Series

The Alpha's Hunger

The Alpha's Promise

The Alpha's Punishment

The Alpha's Protection (Dirty Daddies)

Other Paranormal

The Winter Storm: An Ever After Chronicle

Sci-Fi

Zandian Masters Series

His Human Slave

His Human Prisoner

Training His Human

His Human Rebel

His Human Vessel
His Mate and Master
Zandian Pet
Their Zandian Mate
His Human Possession

Zandian Brides

Night of the Zandians
Bought by the Zandians
Mastered by the Zandians
Zandian Lights
Kept by the Zandian
Claimed by the Zandian
Stolen by the Zandian

Other Sci-Fi

The Hand of Vengeance
Her Alien Masters

ALSO BY LEE SAVINO

Paranormal romance

The Berserker Saga and Berserker Brides (menage werewolves)

These fierce warriors will stop at nothing to claim their mates.

Draekons (Dragons in Exile) with Lili Zander (menage alien dragons)

Crashed spaceship. Prison planet. Two big, hulking, bronzed aliens who turn into dragons. The best part? The dragons insist I'm their mate.

Bad Boy Alphas with Renee Rose (bad boy werewolves)

Never ever date a werewolf.

Tsenturion Masters with Golden Angel

Who knew my e-reader was a portal to another galaxy? Now I'm stuck with a fierce alien commander who wants to claim me as his own.

Contemporary Romance

Royal Bad Boy

I'm not falling in love with my arrogant, annoying, sex god boss. Nope. No way.

Royally Fake Fiancé

The Duke of New Arcadia has an image problem only a fiancé can fix. And I'm the lucky lady he's chosen to play Cinderella.

Beauty & The Lumberjacks

After this logging season, I'm giving up sex. For…reasons.

Her Marine Daddy

My hot Marine hero wants me to call him daddy…

Her Dueling Daddies

Two daddies are better than one.

Innocence: dark mafia romance with Stasia Black

I'm the king of the criminal underworld. I always get what I want. And she is my obsession.

Beauty's Beast: a dark romance with Stasia Black

Years ago, Daphne's father stole from me. Now it's time for her to pay her family's debt…with her body.

ABOUT RENEE ROSE

USA TODAY BESTSELLING AUTHOR RENEE ROSE loves a dominant, dirty-talking alpha hero! She's sold over a million copies of steamy romance with varying levels of kink. Her books have been featured in USA Today's *Happily Ever After* and *Popsugar*. Named Eroticon USA's Next Top Erotic Author in 2013, she has also won *Spunky and Sassy's* Favorite Sci-Fi and Anthology author, *The Romance Reviews* Best Historical Romance, and has hit the *USA Today* list ten times with her Bad Boy Alphas, Chicago Bratva, and Wolf Ranch series.

Renee loves to connect with readers!
www.reneeroseromance.com
reneeroseauthor@gmail.com

ABOUT LEE SAVINO

Lee Savino is a USA today bestselling author, mom and chocoholic.

Warning: Do not read her Berserker series, or you will be addicted to the huge, dominant warriors who will stop at nothing to claim their mates.

I repeat: Do. Not. Read. The Berserker Saga.

Download a free book from www.leesavino.com (don't read that either. Too much hot, sexy lovin').